Blue Dawn Over Gettysburg

A Supernatural Tale of Union Victory

Joe DeSantis

Order this book online at www.trafford.com/07-2396
or email orders@trafford.com

Most Trafford titles are also available at major online book retailers.

Note for Librarians: A cataloguing record for this book is available from Library and Archives Canada at www.collectionscanada.ca/amicus/index-e.html

Printed in Victoria, BC, Canada.

ISBN: 978-1-4251-6748-6

We at Trafford believe that it is the responsibility of us all, as both individuals and corporations, to make choices that are environmentally and socially sound. You, in turn, are supporting this responsible conduct each time you purchase a Trafford book, or make use of our publishing services. To find out how you are helping, please visit www.trafford.com/responsiblepublishing.html

Our mission is to efficiently provide the world's finest, most comprehensive book publishing service, enabling every author to experience success. To find out how to publish your book, your way, and have it available worldwide, visit us online at www.trafford.com/10510

www.trafford.com

North America & international
toll-free: 1 888 232 4444 (USA & Canada)
phone: 250 383 6864 ♦ fax: 250 383 6804
email: info@trafford.com

The United Kingdom & Europe
phone: +44 (0)1865 722 113 ♦ local rate: 0845 230 9601
facsimile: +44 (0)1865 722 868 ♦ email: info.uk@trafford.com

10 9 8 7 6 5 4 3 2

To my Great Uncle Pat

Table of Contents

Background Information

By June of 1863, the American Civil War staggered into its third summer of carnage. Union forces in the Eastern Theater of operations had very little to show for two plus years of blood and sacrifice, while the feared Confederate Army of Northern Virginia was at the very height of its power. Rebel General Robert E. Lee and his troops had beaten numerically superior Federal armies under the generalships of George McClellan in the Seven Days Battle, John Pope at Second Manassas, Ambrose Burnside at Fredericksburg, and Fighting Joe Hooker at Chancellorsville.

Northern morale and support for the war effort was reaching a new low. One more stunning Rebel victory, this time on Union soil, could well have pushed the European powers of England and France to recognize the Confederate States of America as a sovereign nation, perhaps even marking their entrance into the war on behalf of the South. Lee was well aware of the stakes, so much so that he boldly pursued a second invasion of the North from Virginia, through Maryland, and into Pennsylvania.

The 90,000 man Army of the Potomac, which had been placed under the command of General George Meade, himself a Pennsylvania native, eventually discovered the 75,000 man Army of Northern Virginia near of the town of Gettysburg, where arguably the most important battle of the Civil War was fought on July 1st to 3rd of that year. The subsequent

Union victory came at a price of 25,000 Rebel soldiers killed, wounded, captured, or missing in action.

In addition to losing a third of its strength, the Army of Northern Virginia was stripped of invaluable, veteran field officers. The ongoing manpower drain experienced by the Confederacy as the war dragged on insured that it could never replenish the ranks of its most reliable army. As a result, Lee was essentially forced to fight the rest of the war on the defensive, while the Army of Northern Virginia dwindled to a mere 28,000 tattered and starving soldiers by the time they threw down their weapons at Appomattox in April of 1865. The war ended shortly thereafter.

But after so many inglorious defeats, what brought about the sudden Union victory at Gettysburg, the battle that many prominent scholars point to as the turning point of the Civil War? No other battle in the four year conflict has received as much scrutiny, with credit and blame assessed to the participants in equal measure.

This book will reveal a previously unheard of supernatural intervention as the lynchpin to the costly Southern defeat. Vampires have been a part of mankind's collective consciousness for a thousand years, and each country has its own peculiar and bizarre stories of the dreaded night creatures. Who can say with any amount of certainty that they've never interfered in the shaping of the United States?

Chapter 1

First Encounter

The beast weaved its way slowly and silently through the darkened woods, dodging effortlessly around trees and tangled thickets until it stopped before a small clearing. Not 300 feet away stood a shabby, gray-clad picket, who paced unevenly back and forth in front of a pile of felled trees in a dogged effort to stay awake at his post. It was nearly 10PM; in a short time, he would be relieved.

Even at that distance, the beast's senses picked up the scent of the man, covered as he was in dirt and dried sweat, with the lingering aroma of sweet Virginia tobacco emanating from his mouth as he rhythmically breathed in and out. The soldier held an Enfield rifle loosely by his right side, its muzzle tipping downward, nearly touching the ground. He was calm and at peace, but that was soon to change.

The beast trotted low to the ground as it emerged from the woods. It fixed its gaze and quickly picked up speed in a direct line towards the picket, who began to become vaguely uneasy. He stopped his pacing, cocked his head slightly, and peered into the darkness. The man could neither see nor hear anything, yet a feeling of fear and dread began to intensify rapidly within him. He gripped the rifle tightly in both hands as he raised it close to his chest in an unconscious effort to rediscover a sense of security, but there was no relief.

His heart began to pound, and his breathing became short and rapid. The hair on the back of his neck began to tingle, and still the beast flew forward. Finally, the quaking soldier pointed his rifle straight ahead towards the blackness of the open field. He was about to turn and cry out for help just as the beast sprang up from behind the other side of the wooden barricade.

It burned its blazing red stare into the eyes of the picket. The man's frame jerked into a muscle cramped paralysis; his mouth was agape in a futile, silent scream, while his eyes bulged wide in unbelieving terror. There was no escape for him now.

The beast leaped forward, lunged at the statue-like soldier, and instantly enveloped his neck within its jaws. With an effortless jerk to the left, the man's neck snapped like a dry twig as he let out a childlike sigh. He collapsed on his back to the ground while his feet twitched uncontrollably for several seconds. His mouth remained open wide while his tongue settled back into his throat. Glazed eyes stared vacantly up at the night sky; this soldier's small part in the war was over.

The beast coolly motioned passed the lifeless heap and continued on its way, instinctively feeling that it was heading in the right direction. It sniffed the air, sidestepped several armed encampments and soon came towards a road, which it followed undetected in a southeasterly direction by remaining just out of sight in the outlying woods. An old, weather beaten wooden sign that spelled out the name "Cashtown" stood pitched slightly on its side a few yards off the well worn turnpike.

After an uneventful mile of dodging various brigade campfires, the beast came upon a small, three story brick hotel that sat astride the road. The area was bustling with butternut, homespun uniformed infantrymen, irritable teamsters in ramshackle wagons, and dusty artillerists relocating their batteries; they were completing a quick march from nearby Chambersburg.

Two soldiers stood on guard on opposite sides of the hotel's front entrance; directly to their left, a short-staffed white flag ruffled slightly in the warm, summer evening breeze. A closer inspection revealed the upper left hand corner of the flag contained a blue St Andrew's cross with 13 white stars cutting a large X through a squared, red field background. The beast looked up and stared at it with a feverish intensity for several minutes.

A full bearded, slightly built man in a red calico shirt was sitting on the edge of a chair, writing on a rickety table in a far corner of the porch; several soldiers stood crowded around him waiting patiently. He got up slowly and unsteadily, holding a map with one hand and pointing down the pike to the east with the other. The concerned soldiers seemed to be deferring to him. He shook his head slowly up and down several times before thanking and dismissing the men, who all saluted him before leaving. This was a military man of some importance, despite his worn out physical appearance.

At that moment, the beast realized that it had found its mark, but there was no mad rush to the slaughter. On the contrary, it crouched down on all fours and waited patiently just off the edge of the road for several hours, watching as the commotion around the house gradually slackened off to the occasional lone rider passing by. Those soldiers in tents off to the far left and right took to the ground greedily to snatch a few precious hours of sleep before daylight.

It was well past midnight when the guards were relieved by fresh sentries. Minor pleasantries were exchanged for several minutes, and finally the two weary soldiers walked slowly up the road to their company bivouac. They too were anxious for sleep, but they had no idea that fate had just spared them both from an eternal rest.

As the sound of their footsteps grew faint, the beast rose up from its haunches on its two hind legs, its body contorting and changing form within a few moments. It emerged from the darkness and onto the road without hesitation towards the front entrance of the hotel. There was no one about save the two unfortunate guards; they immediately observed the form of an unarmed man walking casually towards them from up the road. He waved his hand to them as he got within talking distance, although his wide brim hat covered his features. The guards assumed he was a local inhabitant, and although they gave him their full attention, they observed his approach without suspicion.

When the stranger got to within a few paces, he slowed, stopped, and raised his head up to expose his face. The last and only thing the soldiers saw were red, animal like eyes piercing a magnetic stare into the back of their brains. Like the unsuspecting picket, neither of them had a moment to make a move or utter a sound. In an instant, the man rushed forward between the two, grabbed each one by the sides of their heads, and then smacked them together. The resultant sound was not unlike the dull crack of an egg shell against the edge of a frying pan.

The sentries immediately went limp, but their bodies did not fall. The stranger grabbed hold of each of them by their hair, then dragged them effortlessly like rag dolls to the woods behind the inn. He pitched them unceremoniously into a nearby culvert, and then carefully covered the bodies with brush and some empty ammunition crates for better concealment.

The grim task completed, the stranger returned quickly to the front of the hotel and placed the soldiers' rifles under the porch. He looked about for stragglers along the road, but all was quiet. Events had thus far gone exceedingly well. He walked quietly to the front door and reached for the white alabaster doorknob.

It mattered not whether the door was locked and bolted. No physical obstruction would have been capable of keeping him out, but at that very moment his hand suddenly stopped just inches short; then it began to tremble uncontrollably. The stranger tried with all his might and strength of will to grasp the doorknob, but deep within, he knew it that it was a useless struggle.

He could not escape the boundaries of his new destiny. He sneered and stared at the door contemptuously. There was now only one avenue available to him, and he had come too far for too long not to attempt such a brazen act.

He positioned himself just inches from the door so that his body would prevent any notice of the missing sentries when it was opened, then he lowered his head once again to allow the brim of his hat to obscure his features. He raised his right hand and knocked three times. After several seconds, he heard hustling and the sound of approaching footsteps, followed by a slightly nauseating aroma that he did not have time to properly identify.

The door was opened by a tall, bootless orderly wearing gray trousers supported by black suspenders, with a somewhat dirty white shirt that was covered with a gray vest. He quickly eyed the stranger up and down, and was more than slightly irritated to have been interrupted by this faceless courier.

"This had better be important," spit the orderly as he tried to suppress his anger from snapping out of a welcome sleep. "Do you realize that we have just now set up camp?"

"I have an urgent message… for the general," replied the stranger with mock excitement.

The orderly sighed. "Yes, yes, they're all important; come in, then" he replied with a tinge of resignation. He had committed a grievous error, assuming that the two outside sentries had already checked the man for proper identification. With an invitation supplied, the stranger lifted his head, intending to lock his gaze on the orderly, but something caught his eye that took him completely by surprise.

The orderly wore a gold pin on the lapel of his vest, but it was no ordinary piece of jewelry. A closer look showed an inverted, V shaped mathematician's compass on the top, followed by a carpenter's square beneath it; in the middle was a capital G. This insignia was meant to announce to all who saw it that the wearer was a Freemason.

The stranger glanced at the pin, blinked, and recoiled for an instant, now recognizing the smell as that of rotting meat. His mind shot back to his recent past, when he had been given an explicit warning to avoid all members of that secret organization. Nevertheless, he stepped into the house to confront his fear, while older memories also began to creep back into his consciousness.

His thoughts drifted back to a time when he was simply John Larson, a bright, fun loving student at the fledgling Agricultural College of Pennsylvania; a young man who had embarked on an exciting scientific journey. But that journey would ultimately become the vehicle for the destruction of his very soul, and soon turned him into a hellish predator that begged no quarter and gave none in return.

Chapter 2

Prelude to Destiny

The young man fidgeted nervously in the red leather chair, looking inquisitively around the sun-drenched room while he waited on pins and needles. He had never been summoned to the President's Office before. It was filled from wall to wall with chemistry and natural science books of all shapes and sizes, along with an interesting array of graphs, charts and laboratory equipment scattered haphazardly about on long, wooden tables that had seen better days.

He strained his neck and scanned the cluttered top of the wide oak desk that loomed directly in front of him like some sacrificial alter, vainly hoping for a faint scrape of information. What infraction had he committed this time to warrant an audience with the head of the college?

He thought long and hard, but he honestly could not recall any one of his numerous student pranks that was truly in bad taste, although his midnight nailing shut of all the outhouse doors elevated him to unprecedented celebrity status, albeit secret.

Could one of his very own school chums have turned him in? If that were the case, would he actually be expelled? What would his parents back in York have to say to such a turn of events? Those sobering thoughts were very unpleasant indeed.

There would not be time to ponder such frightening questions. He heard the sound of a door squeaking open behind him, followed by its

13

swift closing. The young man stiffened and held his breath as the patter of footsteps approached him.

He stared straight ahead, and ultimately decided that if this was to be his last day at the school he loved, then he would conduct himself with dignity...for a change. A soothing voice quickly chimed in on his inner thoughts.

"Ah, Mr. Larson; I gather from your presence that you received my message. That is good."

A handsome, middle aged gentleman in a finely tailored gray suit with a stiff white collar walked passed the young man and nestled comfortably into a high backed chair behind the desk. His dark bearded face, sans moustache, showed no signs of displeasure. On the contrary, he seemed quite pleased as he addressed his captive audience.

"Thank you for coming on such short notice, my lad. I trust that your class schedule has not been interrupted?" There was a short pause.

"No, not at all, Dr. Pugh" countered the now befuddled student, "although I must admit that I was a bit apprehensive when I received the news that you wanted to see me right away. I thought that I might be in some sort of....ah...trouble...sir."

"Trouble?" countered the good doctor in a questioning tone as he began to chuckle. "There is no trouble at all, my boy. In fact, it is just the opposite."

A wave of joy immediately flooded the young man. He let out a long sigh of relief and felt his shoulders drop. All gruesome thoughts of betrayal and punishment also disappeared, although now he was thoroughly puzzled. One was not summoned to the President's office on a whim or pretext. If he had done nothing wrong, what then had he done right? Nothing came to mind.

"I suppose I should tell you the reason for this meeting, Mr. Larson. Let me come straight to the point so that you may return to your classes. An exciting educational opportunity has become available to a select number of our students." He waited to make sure that he had the lad's attention.

"As you are well aware, the College has embraced the advancement of the agricultural theory that has been dubbed, most appropriately I might add, as crop rotation. I trust that you have become fully versed in this soil conservation technique?"

The tone of Pugh's voice inferred that he already knew the answer to his question. His real interest was in the reaction it would bring, and he was not disappointed.

"Yes, sir," the young man chimed in enthusiastically as his face brightened. "It is the planned sequence of changing crops on a yearly basis for the purpose of producing higher yields, and thereby re-introducing needed chemicals back into the soil."

"Quite so, quite so, Mr. Larson," responded a satisfied Pugh. "Here on the college grounds, we have been able to re-affirm this theory on a small scale, but spatial limitations have obviously weakened our case. Do you agree?"

"Yes, sir; larger test areas need to be provided in order to prove this theory once and for all, but I had been told that obtaining more land here is out of the question."

"That is absolutely correct. Fiscal constraints and inflexible adjoining landowners have damaged our efforts, to be sure. However, an alternative plan to the actual purchase of additional property was proposed at a faculty meeting several months ago, and I am happy to announce that we have reached a consensus on a suitable solution."

Dr. Pugh paused for a moment, and then leaned forward in his chair.

"My questions for you, Mr. Larson, are quite simple. First, are you interested in learning more; second, and most important of all, would you like to lend your assistance in this exciting new venture?

"Absolutely, to both questions," the excited student blurted out. "I would be willing to help in any way possible."

"That is the reply I had hoped for," Pugh responded. "Now that I have enlisted your aid without reservation, I believe that I should tell you of the actual plan." He nestled in his seat like a chicken on her eggs.

"I have written to the owners of a number of large farms and plantations throughout the country, inquiring to see if they would be interested in testing the crop rotation theory on their various properties. This would then provide us with a more comprehensive feedback on a large scale basis, while simultaneously increasing the profits of the owners. Are you with me so far?"

"Yes, sir; I am. It sounds like an excellent plan."

"I am glad that you are in agreement with us," responded Pugh as he tried to suppress mild amusement of the lad's wholehearted seal of approval.

"We would send a promising student to each location to help formulate, implement, and monitor the crop rotations for a period of nine months; it would be the duty of each student to send regular, monthly reports to his professor, and upon return to the College, to remain in contact with his respective property owner for the purpose of obtaining yield results for final analysis."

"It has been our good fortune to receive favorable replies from owners in five states——, Massachusetts, New York, Maryland, Illinois, and......Louisiana." The hesitation in naming the final state did not go unnoticed by young Larson. He raised his eyebrows and waited for further information.

"Of course," Pugh continued, almost apologetically, "you are undoubtedly well aware that Louisiana is deep in the South. Sectional differences of late have resulted in strained relations on both sides of the Mason Dixon Line."

"Of that I am sure, sir," countered the attentive student. "The person sent there may certainly have a more difficult time, particularly if he were a Northerner by birth."

"Undoubtedly," replied Pugh resignedly as he shifted uncomfortably in his chair. "Let me be blunt. You have been chosen by faculty consensus to be one of the five students to take part in the study. That is the good news." Larson could hardly believe his ears; his mouth opened in surprise at the sound of his good fortune.

"However," countered Pugh, "of your fellow classmates, Richard Hope has been slated for New York, Warren Sullivan for Massachusetts, Michael Fitzmaurice for Illinois, and Lawrence Murphy for Maryland." There was a short pause.

"And now for the bad news; that leaves you, John, a native Pennsylvanian, for Louisiana, which I do not have to remind you, is a slave state that opted for secession this past January." The president looked at the young student carefully.

"Do you have reservations about undertaking such a formidable task, in light of the fact that your state has vociferously voiced its criticism of the institution of slavery? Southerners are quite adamant on the subject, you know, and tend to let their passions run away with them. Your stay may certainly prove somewhat uncomfortable, particularly if the memory of our Congressman Wilmot's Proviso has not faded away. He created quite a firestorm when he proposed that slavery should be excluded from all lands garnered from the late war with Mexico."

"I will attempt to faithfully steer clear of the subject of slavery at all times sir, in spite of the obvious examples of inhumanity that will certainly be displayed throughout my stay. What is more troubling to me personally is this secession business. No one knows how it will all play out with the Southern states. I simply cannot believe that our country will split apart like this."

He shook his head dejectedly and paused for a moment before continuing. "Nevertheless… I would be a guest in someone's home, and I would certainly do nothing to disgrace the good name of the College, to be sure."

"That is what I was hoping you might say, young man," Pugh replied happily. "It's settled then. Your destination will be a Cajun plantation by the name of Etenel Babako; it lies just outside of Baton Rouge. It is nicely situated on the banks of the Mississippi River, and is quite impressive, according to descriptions from its owner. You should have ample acreage to conduct your field tests."

"This sounds like a wonderful opportunity, Dr. Pugh. I will not let you down, sir," the young man said solemnly. "When am I scheduled to begin?"

"You will leave on April 6th. Travel plans have been pre-arranged for you," he said in a somewhat embarrassed tone. "I went under the assumption that you would say yes, my boy. The better part of your journey will be by rail, so hopefully you should experience only relatively minor inconveniences. Those Dixie fire eaters have done nothing substantial as of yet to disrupt interstate travel, but there's just no telling what they will try next because of this secession talk."

"If all goes well, it should take you the better part of a week to reach Baton Rouge and Mr. Jacques Dumaine, the owner with whom I have corresponded. He seems keenly interested in improving his crop yield, and is open to any suggestions that you may lay out before him."

John suddenly began to comprehend the totality of the situation; he sat silent for several seconds. "Then this will all take place within a month's time." He hesitated, and then continued. "I have never been out of Pennsylvania before, Doctor; I must write to my parents in York to obtain their permission for such a long journey from the school. They may very well object to this."

Pugh's embarrassed tone resurfaced yet again. "I ...have already taken the liberty of writing your parents a short while ago, my boy. They too are most anxious for you to take part in this rare opportunity, although I asked them to remain silent until the proper time."

Dr. Pugh then looked at him sternly. "Of course, the increased distance from them should not be used as an excuse; they are expecting you to write regularly, none the less. I seem to recall that they expressed some marked irritation over your continued lack of personal correspondence."

John let out a wince, and shook his head sheepishly. "Ah...that is correct sir. I will write to them tonight. I promise."

"That is a capital idea, Mr. Larson, considering the fact that you have only four weeks before you leave on your assignment." He paused for a moment to let the suggestion sink in.

"Now, off you go to see Professor MacDonald. He will fill you in on all of the particulars of your journey, and also go over the all important list of materials and equipment that you will need to take with you. Once you are in Louisiana, you will be, for all intents and purposes, on your own. I am sure that he will be of great help to you in your preparation."

Dr. Pugh rose from his chair and extended his hand over the desk. "I believe that covers just about everything, Mr. Larson, other than to say that I wish you good luck in your assignment. I am supremely confident that this will prove quite an experience for you, young man."

"I am positive that it will sir;" John replied gratefully. "Thank you ever so much for this unique opportunity."

Dr. Evan Pugh could never have imagined in his wildest nightmares that the experience he spoke of so highly would seal his eager young student's fate for all eternity.

Chapter 3

The Journey Begins

John could hardly believe his sudden bout of good fortune as he left Dr. Pugh's office nestled neatly within the bowels of the seven story brick building that was known simply as the "Old Main." His mind raced frantically to cover the flurry of activities that had to be performed prior to his departure.

The next three plus weeks seemed to vanish in a whirlwind of studying, packing, letter writing, and securing the proper laboratory equipment, not to mention the obligatory round of farewells to his classmates. There were also several meetings with his advisor and the other four lucky student trip participants relative to coordinating individual field experiments and data recording.

Douglas MacDonald was a thin, demanding, gray haired old salt of a professor, but he was also generous with his time and experience. The students were all well aware that he expected neat, clear, concise reports in monthly intervals. They were eager not to disappoint him, or to incur his wrath despite the safe but temporary cushion of distance that their locales would provide. After all, in nine months, they would be back, and if he was displeased, they would have to face the dire consequences.

Even from afar, MacDonald was not one to trifle with. "Remember, gentlemen," he said sternly in a gravely voice, "your monthly reports shall be my gauge of your field work. Of particular importance will be the advice that you provide to your respective hosts regarding the improvement of their soil based upon the data your initial tests reveal."

He continued on. "These reports, coupled with the final yield results received from the property owners, will determine your actual grade for this unique assignment. More importantly, the Agricultural College will obtain vital information to further the advancement of soil conservation for the betterment of all."

The students were completely aware of the significance of the opportunity, but in order to reassure their instructor one last time, they solemnly shook their heads in agreement, and pledged to do their best.

Finally, departure day arrived for the "fortunate five," as they had become referred to by their fellow classmates. After a final briefing by Professor MacDonald, which included distribution of their individual trip schedules and various transport tickets, the young men were dismissed to begin the journey to their respective states. But there was a surprise on hand for John.

"Just one moment Mr. Larson, if you please," MacDonald spoke softly. John stopped dead in his tracks. The others filed quickly out of the room, uneasy with the uncharacteristically soothing sound of the professor's voice. It was something that they were not used to, and the other boys were thrilled not to be singled out. They liked John, but not enough to wait around for him in this instance; lest they too became subjects of individual attention by the teacher they called "The Meat Grinder."

MacDonald waited until the other students had left the room before continuing. "John, your trip is certainly the longest, as I am sure you've surmised. With that in mind, Dr. Pugh and I thought it would be fitting that you be allowed a short visit with your family in York. After all, it is on the stage route to Baltimore, where you will board the train for your academic journey, so to speak. Consider it a small bonus from the College for the added inconveniences you will suffer."

Upon feigning a hearty thank you to Professor MacDonald, John exited with a feeling of deep uneasiness. He had not been on good terms with his father for several years. As the boy had grown into a young man, the usual conflicts between father and son had developed, and they had not yet been resolved.

Hugh Larson was a forceful man used to having his way, in his own household and in a court of law. John bristled under his dominance, and while his mother was sympathetic to her only child's situation, she invariably sided reluctantly with her husband. Hugh had hoped that his son would follow in his footsteps and join his law practice in York, but his son was steadfastly bound and determined to be a scientist in a profession of his own choosing.

A rare victory for the young man to attend the college of his choice only served to widen the distance between them. John sensed deep down that his mother must have finally stood her ground on such an important matter, although she never admitted to it. He was thankful for her efforts on his behalf, but the distasteful episode found her trapped in the middle of a struggle between two strong willed individuals. She would grow bitter and resent them both as time passed.

John immediately decided that he would indeed follow school orders by taking the coach route southeast through Harrisburg and into York, but the idea of a brief family reunion was totally out of the question. He would continue straight on through to the rail line in Baltimore, ending the first leg of a journey that the 19 year old hoped would be an exciting personal and professional experience.

The preliminary daybreak coach ride itself proved to be a very dusty and jaw shattering affair. John's constant worry throughout the trip was the ongoing condition of the delicate scientific equipment provided by the college. Martin Marshall, the foul mouthed, Irish, tobacco spitting driver provided by the coach line, made little effort for the comfort and well being of his passengers, let alone their accompanying baggage.

His seemingly endless expressions of profanity, aimed principally at the horses, were no doubt garnered after many years of intense personal study in the old country, and he secretly reveled in raising the eyebrows of his startled customers. "Beggin' yur pardn ta be shurrr" he would say to the travelers as they winced in synch with his swearing. On this journey, besides John, there were the three ancient, dowager-like Gavaghan sisters, along with a portly, congenial businessman named Timothy Dolph.

While never intentionally riding over ruts and depressions in the road, Marshall certainly made no great effort to avoid them. John tensed after every jolt, as visions of broken test tubes and bent weighing scales danced in his head. What if much of the equipment became damaged en route? How would he be able to properly conduct his tests? How would Professor MacDonald react? He couldn't wait to reach Baltimore and the safety of the train.

The sadistic coachman seemed to find it perversely enjoyable to watch the poor lad hop out and breathlessly rip open his large trunk at every rest interval to check for damage. Fortunately, there was no breakage of any kind, although John attributed that more to the careful planning and packaging by Professor MacDonald, plus sheer luck, than to the skill of his driver.

After passing Lewiston and Harrisburg, the coach made its scheduled stop in York. The dazed passengers happily stumbled out; the

Gavaghans stretched their creaking legs and looked around intently for a place to freshen up, not that it would have helped very much, while Mr. Dolph quietly walked down a nearby alleyway and unceremoniously relieved himself behind a rose bush.

John watched the proceedings with some degree of amusement. "Yes," he whispered softly, "for men, the world is our toilet." But he himself could not leave the coach for fear of being recognized by one of the locals, or worse, by a relative. A situation like that would have forced a short visit home to his parents despite his wishes.

His lower back begged for a respite, so he sank on his knees to the floorboard and stretched straight up until his joints popped. After the pain subsided, he sat up and leaned back while closing the window curtain. The 20 minute rest stop was unnerving, but the coach finally got under way without any sightings by friends or family.

After several more hours on the road, the coach arrived in the city of Baltimore, and not a moment too soon to suit John. He pleaded with the driver not to unload his equipment trunk, a request that delighted Marshall to no end. John rescued it from the carriage and rested it gently on the ground, his body slumped in relief. At the same moment, his personal suitcase came crashing down into a cloud of dust not two feet from him.

He jerked his head upwards in a start and looked up at the dirty, smiling face of his soon to be ex-tormentor. The driver proceeded to spit a large brown wad of tobacco on the rear of one of his horses, and then he bade John good luck and Godspeed on the remainder of his trip. Oddly enough, John was fairly sure that the man meant it despite the constant teasing. In any case, he was glad to be rid of Marshall and headed to the train station.

John had never been on a train before, but he was confident that it would be child's play by comparison. Unfortunately, the second leg of the journey did not prove to be the magic carpet ride of steel that John had envisioned, although he had to admit that his precious equipment trunk was in the infinitely safer environment of the train's baggage car; for that he was very thankful.

The first class car notwithstanding, general creature comforts for passengers on the Baltimore and Ohio Railroad would have been described as Spartan at best. Leaving the cold April air at the station for a thinly padded seat in passenger car #2 did little to warm John's bones. There was but a single wood burning stove in the middle of the car, and the seating area on either side had been quickly taken by more knowledgeable train riders.

The stove was stoked and filled periodically by a seemingly ancient looking Negro, who had a chair placed beside the car's hand brake. John wondered if the old man truly had enough physical strength to slow the car down if any track problems arose. He sincerely doubted it, and he tried to forget about that frightening scenario by gazing out the window at the passing scenery.

Surprisingly, the train did not run as fast as John had envisioned. Its speed seemed to top out at a rate of about 15 miles covered in an hour's time, so he was able to observe a good deal from his window seat. He would have been on edge had he known that the slower speed was a hedge against possible collisions with other trains, not to mention the engineer's decided lack of faith in the track's tensile strength. In this instance, ignorance was bliss.

The passengers huddled in car #2 were certainly a mixed bag of travelers, but the one common denominator was their race; all were white, except for Sam, the old brakeman/stove stoker. As the train stopped to refuel the tenders at designated wood stations along the line, burly black men were waiting expectantly to load up whatever amount was necessary for the seemingly insatiable locomotive.

It suddenly struck John that these poor unfortunates were in all probability slaves of the railroad line. He shot a glance back at Sam, who sat in his chair with a somewhat sad expression, staring sadly into space. Maryland had certainly not shown itself to be very enthusiastic for the Northern "points of view" of late. In truth, the city of Baltimore itself was a hotbed of activity, filled with Southern sympathizers who openly expressed their dissatisfaction with the federal government.

As a native Pennsylvanian, John never had a great deal of interaction with slaves throughout his young life, although he did come into contact with free Negroes from time to time. He made a mental note that once he crossed into Virginia and pushed further South, the sight of slaves and their masters would be a daily occurrence; for that he would have to be prepared.

While en route to Louisiana and his temporary plantation home, John was constantly reminded that train travel left a great deal to be desired. The ride became filled with lurches and sudden stops, often courtesy of slow moving wagons crossing the tracks, or wandering livestock from adjacent farms along the way. The triangular cow catcher at the head of the engine performed admirably, although more than a few farmers were thoroughly dissatisfied with the physical damage done to some of their four legged property.

The most annoying aspect of the journey was the never-ending parade of railroad companies that seemed to spring up suddenly along the way, courtesy of the Southern propensity towards privatization of its rail lines. Upon arrival in Washington, John was informed that he was to board a different train and that he was now the guest of the Orange and Alexandria Railroad.

But that was far from the end of his rail travel introduction, as the train snaked its way southwest through a short laundry list of towns and cities. Lynchburg was the initial site of the annoying Southern railroad ritual of stopping a few miles outside of a town, leaving the train, and then boarding an equally uncomfortable one that was waiting on that portion of the track belonging to a rival line; with a bit of luck, passengers' baggage would be placed on board also.

John found out that he was now on the Virginia and Tennessee Railroad; upon arriving in Bristol, the East Tennessee and Virginia Railroad appeared around a bend. In Knoxville, the East Tennessee and Georgia Railroad welcomed him with open arms, while the Memphis and Charleston was waiting patiently in Stevenson.

The rails turned westward as the Mississippi Central at Grand Junction, then south to Jackson, where the New Orleans, Jackson, and Great Northern Railroad brought him passed Lakes Maurepas and Pontchartrain into the grand, old city of New Orleans. Obviously, with each new rail company signaling a drop off and pick up, keeping up with the lines' name changes was the least of John's worry. He soon learned to put them out of his mind entirely, and he concentrated on making sure that his trunks were loaded on board with each train change.

When John complained bitterly to an engineer on the Mississippi Central, the surprised veteran employee smiled broadly, but told him in no uncertain terms to count his blessings. "Consider yourself extremely fortunate that your particular route utilizes a five inch rail gauge track from start to finish, young man; otherwise, you would have been forced to change trains even more frequently to accommodate the differences in gauge width."

John shook his head in disbelief. He could not comprehend how such an unproductive system could spring up and be allowed to flourish on such a grand scale, but he did not dwell on it for very long. An unhappy rail experience that had started five days ago out of Baltimore, one that included sleeping fitfully on the trains en route, ended in the late afternoon, and he wandered wide eyed about the famous French Quarter dragging his baggage noisily behind him.

He found cheap lodging for the night on Decatur Street, but wound up pining for the relative safety of his room later in the evening. The local inhabitants, both men and women, were a bit too free in their comportment to suit his taste. While walking in the Vieux Carre, John felt as though he stuck out in the Bohemian looking crowd, particularly when he stopped briefly on the corner of Bourbon and Bienville Streets and entered an establishment simply referred to as the "Coffee House."

He soon became fairly confident that this saloon would not prove beneficial to his overall good health; it seemed to draw both bizarre and dangerous looking waterfront types of all shapes, colors, and sizes. There was a silent, solitary old woman in particular who stared at him intently from across the room; she was a mulatto, with curly salt and pepper hair, shining black eyes, and a ruffled red dress that partially hid a small pouch tied around her waist. The wary patrons gave her ample space.

Rather than attempt to discover the reason for this undue attention, John decided that discretion would be the better part of valor; he exited the establishment and made a bee line for his lodging house. But he noticed that the female stranger had also departed and was following him at a respectable distance. He began to feel uneasy.

Finally, as he reached Decatur Street, John took advantage of a large group of revelers coming from the opposite direction; he cut between them and slipped down the entrance of a dark alleyway to await his pursuer. When the old woman reached the alleyway, she stopped, peered into the darkness, and addressed him. "Do not fear me, boy," she bleated. "I am here to help you. Come out now." John spoke while slowly emerging from the shadows. "What is it you want of me? I have no money to spare, if begging is your aim."

The woman reached for her pouch and placed a hand inside. For an instant, John thought that she would flash a pistol for a robbery, but instead, she pulled out a small bottle along with some dried twigs and offered them to John. "Holy wahter…from da cathedral, wit' some hawthorn an' mountain ash; take dem an' keep dem close always."

John waived them off. "And why would I need any of that?'

The old woman bowed her head and responded ominously; "Dere is a sad destiny ahead… should you continue on dis path. De aura is about you. Take great care, boy."

John gave her an incredulous look, and she responded in kind. "I be known roun' here as Marie Laveau. I…know of such things. May the Virgin Mary protect you."

She then turned and quickly made her way back towards the center of the French Quarter. John stood stunned for a moment, then raced to his second floor room and locked the door. He could hardly wait for morning and the resumption of his journey.

Chapter 4

The Last Chance

Daylight came not a moment too soon for young Larson. The night air had filled his ears with the resounding sounds of laughter, shouts, curses, and gunshots. When he reached the street for a short walk to his waiting stagecoach at Vieux Carre, he looked into the faces of the passersby, many of whom were wandering slowly about with puffy, half shut eyes.

He wondered whether they were innocents like himself, whose sleep had been thoroughly disrupted by the bawdy crowds, or if they were actual culprits suffering the just rewards for their night revelries. And then there was the old woman to consider.

Why was she so interested in him? Just the thought of her gaze upon him sent a quick shiver down his spine. There was something unsettling about her words, and the strange gifts she offered, especially the holy water, brought a mixture of puzzlement and fear. It was an understatement that this trip was not unfolding as he had envisioned.

John arrived at the depot and handed his luggage to the waiting coachman, who secured the baggage with great care. This caused him to become cautiously optimistic about the delicate instruments; but what brought a great sigh of relief were the elliptical springs attached to the front and rear wheels. Perhaps this would not be a duplication of the bone shattering coach ride that he was forced to endure from the college.

Shortly after boarding the carriage, he was joined by two other travelers—a short, aging, well dressed Southern gentleman sporting a neatly pressed white suit, and his noticeably younger wife, whose plump figure cast a great shadow over him. Her constant, high pitched chatter soon dampened John's initial euphoria, and he became sadly convinced that he would experience an unpleasant ride after all.

The coach clattered out of the crescent city southwest onto the busy River Road, where the obligatory social introductions commenced. The unlikely looking couple was Mr. James Noonan, a prominent Southern banker, and his carping, shrewish wife, Lucinda. It seemed that they had been visiting relatives and some prospective clients in New Orleans, and were on their way home to Baton Rouge.

Mrs. Noonan was as talkative as her husband was quiet. Her steady stream of questions followed with such rapidity that John was oblivious to the fact that this female stranger had soon learned more about him than anyone else save his parents. By the time he realized what had happened, the damage was done. Sensing that she held a captive audience, the woman droned on, offering her opinions from his future professional plans to his personal ones as well.

It seemed that she had a lovely young niece named Tallulah, the daughter of a well respected family in Natchitoches, whom she thought would be a perfect match for John. While he had never been particularly comfortable on the idea of such arranged meetings, the initial description provided by Mrs. Noonan sounded quite promising. Perhaps he could mix a little business with romance here in the South while out on loan so to speak from the college, and also develop some social contacts that might prove beneficial to his future career plans.

However, while beginning to stammer out an affirmative reply, John inadvertently shot Mr. Noonan a quick glance, and saw the man quickly shake his head firmly from side to side with his lips pursed shut, as though he were ready to burst with disgust. The decision was finalized on the spot; John politely feigned mild interest, with an insincere promise to keep in touch.

A look of undying gratitude must have passed over John's face as he nodded to Mr. Noonan, because the old man responded by forcibly suppressing a laugh, as though he thoroughly understood the poor boy's situation, and his relief.

While Lucinda was an uncontrollable chatterbox, to her credit she was also a wealth of information. John was astounded by the sights of the gorgeous plantation homes that lined the route along the Mississippi, one seemingly more spectacular than the next. Mrs. Noonan easily rattled off the names of each one, while also providing the requisite family histories of all who resided therein, including the scandals.

Her background information of the magnificent structures and grounds with names like Destrehan, Glendale, Felicity, Ashland, Evergreen, and Tally-Ho brought a steady stream of superlatives from the young man's lips, although he candidly admitted that he knew very little about the subject of architecture. John looked dreamily out the coach window and wondered aloud if his temporary home would be as beautiful as those he was witnessing on the ride to it.

Such an opening was too good to be ignored. Lucinda chimed in rapidly with an air of haughty confidence. "Etenel Babako takes a back seat to no other plantation in Louisiana, young man. That is the name of the plantation where you will be staying. As a matter of fact, I have found it to be one of the most breathtaking places in the entire South, if I do say so myself. Don't you agree James?"

The old man was caught off guard. His mind was elsewhere, as was usually the case when his wife was speaking. "Agree? Why, ah…. yes, absolutely" he said cautiously as his voice trailed off, hoping not to have agreed to something that would come back later to bite him in the ass.

"I have accompanied James there for business reasons on a number of occasions, and I must say that the interior of the main house is absolutely stunning. Unfortunately, I have not had the pleasure of any extended conversations with your future host, Mr. Dumaine, but he is a proper Southern gentleman, I can assure you. You will want for nothing during your stay."

"That is very reassuring, Mrs. Noonan. Thank you," replied John.

"Call me Lucinda, dear. After all, we could be family someday."

"Yes…..family," John managed with a weak smile as he conjured up an image of Tallulah as some repulsive Dixie Harpy. Mr. Noonan stared out the window and said nothing, but his silence and stone face spoke volumes.

The remainder of the trip was marked chiefly by the woman's incessant banter. John attempted to negate the noise by focusing on the beautiful River Road scenery, but invariably his attention was pulled back into the confines of the carriage by loud, repeated inquiries from Lucinda.

He could not even use the pretext of pretending to fall sleep to escape his predicament. Mr. Noonan had already wisely pursued that avenue of escape, one that he had no doubt perfected over years of trial and error. It would be in poor taste for both male companions to nod off for a few winks, even if she did deserve it. Besides, she would merely wake up her husband, and John owed him a favor.

Finally, the carriage rounded a short bend, and slowed to a stop as its dust billowed about. "Etenel Babako," the stork-like coachman announced with an air of formality. John poked his head eagerly out the window and was met by a breathtaking sight.

Just off the main road were two towering rows of massive oaks trees planted long ago on either side of a greenbelt pathway. Their canopies, dripping profusely with Spanish moss, bent inward and became intertwined; they formed a green, funnel like atmosphere that blocked out much of the sunlight beneath them.

Flanked on either side of the tree rows were spacious bowling greens, while set behind each green was an orchard. A mansion stood centered proudly behind the end lines of the oak trees; only its central portions could be seen in the distance. The rest was blocked out by the trunks and wide branches of the oaken sentinels.

However, John could make out large, white columns set in front of what appeared to be an immaculate, three storied, red brick mansion. He unconsciously whistled in awe as he bounded from the carriage and eagerly proceeded to gather his belongings. Lucinda remained in the coach and tendered a long goodbye that John barely took notice of. He was nearly free, although the same could not be said for Mr. Noonan.

He was surprised, however, when the old man got out and approached him with a look of concern. A wave of his hand motioned John away from the coach, and the straining ears of Lucinda, whose head appeared out the window in a shameless effort to overhear the impending conversation. When they reached a comfortable distance, Mr. Noonan turned towards John to speak.

"I wish you the best in all of your future endeavors, young man. I am sure that you will meet with success in whatever path you may choose to follow." It was here that he paused, and then forced himself to continue with an air of halting reluctance.

"Your prospective host, Mr. Dumaine, is a very successful planter, even by Louisiana standards. As my wife has made mention, I have been to this estate for brief visits to go over his accounts and various banking issues. I have always found him to be... an intelligent... persuasive.... and ....well bred individual." Noonan then opened his mouth as though wanting to continue, but no words came forth. He looked directly at the main house with an icy stare.

"Etenel Babako is truly a world unto itself. It is largely self-sufficient, with enough resources to keep it isolated and forgotten....as if that was what someone had intended." He paused once more and looked at the ground, as though fighting to get the proper words out.

"Mr. Dumaine is also... a very private....even secretive person. While I have never had reason to fear him, nevertheless, I have always left his plantation with a deep sense of relief." He turned his attention back to John and spoke with a sincerity that the young man had never experienced, even with his own father.

"My home in Baton Rouge is no more than two hours hard ride from here. If you should feel the need for a change in locale, my home is at your disposal. I am sure that this would not jeopardize your ongoing field work." John was dumbfounded; he stood silent for several seconds, and then responded thoughtfully.

"Thank you very much, Mr. Noonan. It is a gracious invitation, to be sure, but I must respectfully decline. I fear that my host might take offense to such an arrangement, and as a representative of the college, I have assured my professors that I would do nothing to impugn its reputation. I would also be hard pressed to fulfill my research within the proper time frame traveling back and forth; approximately four hours per day would be lost. That would not be practical, under the circumstances, sir."

"Yes, yes of course," Noonan said dejectedly. "Nevertheless, if you should need help or guidance of any kind, please do not hesitate to contact me. Please say you will do so."

"I shall, sir," John blurted out incredulously. "It has been a distinct pleasure to share a coach with you and your wife, sir."

With that, Noonan shook the young man's hand vigorously, and returned to the company of his impatient wife within the carriage. As the coachman shut the door, John unconsciously gritted his teeth; he heard the shrill tones of Lucinda as she peppered her husband with questions of their conversation. John picked up his luggage and began the long walk down the shaded, well worn footpath between the oak rows.

The coach slowly took up speed and continued west on the River Road towards Baton Rouge. Mr. Noonan deflected his wife's Spanish Inquisition, an ongoing necessity on his part that infuriated her to no end. He deftly concocted a vague "man to man" type of discussion with John that soothed his wife's curiosity, if not her anger. With the episode laid to rest, he soon resumed his persona as the sleeping traveler.

Nevertheless, he was struck by one of John's statements, and he could not help but reply to it, if only to himself. "You fear of upsetting your host, young man. I pray that is the only thing you fear during your stay."

Chapter 5

A Rude Introduction

The noonday sun danced in and out of the stretching green branches on the live oaks as John continued his walk towards the main house. Oddly enough, there were no signs of movement in any direction he looked, which seemed completely out of character for a 1,000 acre establishment. He was under the distinct impression that Southern plantations were small towns unto themselves, continuously bustling with activity at all hours of the day until well into the evening.

While his initial reaction concerning the trees looming above him was that of fascination, it took a decidedly darker turn as he ventured further away from the main road. A closer inspection showed that they had distinctively gnarled, disjointed shapes, almost as though each one had its own personality. The original intent of the plantings was surely meant to provide a grand, green corridor of comfort for a visitor approaching the mansion.

Somehow, that had changed dramatically over the years. The stately oaks now seemed to resemble mammoth wrists that had desperately burst forth from the earth, while the main branches had morphed into elongated hands clutching wildly in all directions, waiting patiently to ensnare an unsuspecting victim walking below.

John felt increasingly apprehensive as he worked his way down the worn, dirt path. He attempted to shift his concentration from his immediate surroundings to the beautiful home that lay straight ahead; it unconsciously represented a safe harbor. He quickened his pace despite carrying his luggage in one hand, while dragging and jostling the large trunk along the ground with the other. Any thoughts of the delicate, technical equipment packed within were summarily dismissed in favor of his image of reaching the front door of the mansion.

As he got to within shouting distance of the house, a figure stepped out stiffly from behind one of the trees, causing John to let out a short yelp and nearly freeze in mid stride. "You are Larson, yes?" the man asked in a flat, disinterested voice that was tinged with what sounded very much like a French accent. "We have been expecting your arrival. I am Algernon, the head overseer."

John was put off by the dramatic entrance and less than gracious tonal inflection, but he made a great effort to mask his immediate displeasure while quickly eyeing the man up and down. This Algernon wore a white, wide-brimmed hat, blue striped shirt, and dark brown pants, which were held up over his ample belly by a large, black leather belt with a gold buckle. The man possessed only average height at best, but he portrayed a swagger of immense self importance.

While the overseer might have been considered handsome in his day, middle age had not treated him with any great kindness. Wrinkles stretched over his face to his brown eyes, and his dark hair had lost much of its sheen. This was certainly a man who had seen his best years, although he probably did not realize it, or would not admit it.

"It is certainly a relief and a pleasure to have finally arrived at my destination, sir. Your plantation is quite beautiful."

"It is not MY plantation," the man responded brusquely. "As I said, I am the head overseer. Mr. Dumaine is the owner of Etenel Babako. He is currently ...away on personal business. You shall see him tonight, however. In the meantime, I will attend to your needs." He turned towards the main house, cupped his hands around his mouth, and let out a yell. "Williiee. Williieeeeee. Come here at once."

A young, ragged looking Negro boy of about 12 bounded out from behind the front door. He ran up to John without speaking or looking up and grabbed the luggage bag and trunk. The boy then dragged them gingerly around the side of the house and disappeared from view.

John thought the boy's actions very strange. If he were to be a guest of Mr. Dumaine, as per the arrangements, why then were his belongings not taken directly into the main house? Algernon could see quite clearly that the young man was puzzled, and he was quick to respond.

"Your travel bag and equipment are being taken to the garconniere," he said with more than a bit of haughty satisfaction; he was confident that the young man had no idea to what he was referring.

"I must admit that I am at a loss, sir," John responded honestly, self conscious that he had never mastered any foreign languages, as his mother had often begged him to.

"It is what you AMERICANS would call…a guest house," replied the overseer condescendingly. "It is behind the main house on the left. Would you prefer to have your lunch now, or go on a brief tour of the plantation before Mr. Dumaine's arrival this evening?

John ignored the continued show of rude behavior and concentrated hard on keeping a civil tongue in his head. "I had a very hearty breakfast this morning, sir. Actually, I would be more interested in a tour of the grounds, if it would not be too much trouble."

"Mr. Dumaine has instructed me to make you familiar with all of our operations. I will have a carriage brought up at once."

With that, Algernon quickly spun around and trailed off in the same direction as the missing Willie, leaving John to complete his short walk to the mansion alone. The absence of Southern hospitality notwithstanding, he was thoroughly impressed with the grace and beauty of the building that stood proudly before him.

There were 10 white columns fronting the building; they appeared to be reasonable facsimiles of an ancient Greek temple, while an open balcony on the second floor invited one to sample the cool evening breezes. Five dormered white windows sat astride a sloped, gabled roof, with two red bricked chimneys centered at the peak.

Upon finishing his visual survey of the front portion of the house, John was about to walk around to the rear when the ubiquitous Algernon reappeared. The young man continued in a half hearted attempt to cozy up to his temporary host, despite the feeling that his prospects for success were marginal at best.

"I am very impressed with this building, sir," he said haltingly. "The craftsmanship is exquisite. Exactly what is the purpose of the large painted screens on both ends of the house?"

"You mean the JALOUSIES," Algernon responded with emphasis and continued pomposity. "They shield the outdoor stairways that lead to the upper floors."

"Oh," replied John as he stepped onto the front porch. He then deliberately turned away, trying desperately to hide his rising anger. "Americans might call them SHUTTERS," he said in a rising voice. "Are you going to invite me inside, or must I wait for a written invitation?"

Algernon was startled, but recovered and replied excitedly at the prospect of a verbal sparring match. "Mr. Dumaine will have the pleasure of escorting you personally through the interior portions of the house.

Rest assured that you will be suitably .....entertained. Ah, Joshua is finally arriving from the stable with the carriage." He turned and let out a withering yell. "Hurry up, damn you, while there is still daylight left."

The slow clatter of hoofs brought a large work cart pulled by two ancient, flea bitten horses; they were lead gently by an equally old looking black man. The overseer climbed up onto the driver's seat without another word, while John scampered up and sat on his right.

"Thank you," John said matter of factly to the old man, who looked surprised but pleased by the acknowledgement.

"There is no need to thank slaves for their work, Mr. Larson" growled the overseer. "You are no longer in Pennsylvania."

John sadly shook his head and let out a deep sigh of disgust. "I can see that quite clearly without a reminder from you, sir. The tour, if you please."

There was a short, uncomfortable silence as the cart clattered its way to the right around the main house, passed the still dormant apple orchard along a rutted dirt road no more than 15 feet wide. A thicket of woods blocked their view on the left.

"Etenel Babako is our jewel on the Mississippi, Mr. Larson. It is well over 1,000 acres, and every acre has a prescribed function. If you look to your right, the privy, as YOU would call it, is hidden just beyond the orchard near a small stream. Farther off to the right you will see the stables and barn; it has an attached, fully functioning blacksmith shop behind it, along with a fair sized henhouse. The chickens provide the darkies with their ration of meat. No need to spoil them further with anything else."

They continued their way slowly down the access road toward the river, and soon came upon two other structures that were placed nearly side by side. The first looked remarkably similar to the mansion itself. It was about a 25 foot square, single story, red brick house, but without the white columns and window dormers. The overseer resumed his speech.

"This is the garconniere." John had grown tired of his tour guide's word games and shot him a wicked, fiery glance. It was thoroughly successful, considering their close proximity.

"The guest house," Algernon relayed somewhat meekly as he turned away. He cleared his throat quietly before describing the simple wooden shed close by.

"This is the...pigeon house," he spit out slowly, as though he dearly wanted to give it its French name, but decided to avoid further hostility. John smiled contentedly.

After a distance of about 100 yards, they came upon a slightly elevated field. John scanned it quickly; he did not need his driver to name the crop that would fill these acres. The stubble and remnants of the previous year brought back memories of Pennsylvania.

"Corn," John said wistfully. "I hope to see how Louisiana corn measures up that of my native state, sir. Pennsylvanians are quite proud of their sweet corn. I take it the structures coming up are the mill and storage barn?"

"Correct, sir," Algernon replied, rather surprised at the young man's horticultural knowledge, "but I do not think you will recognize our remaining crops."

The cart plodded forward, and eventually began to make its way beside what first appeared to be flooded acreage. Slaves dotted these low lying fields, gathering up crayfish by the hundreds from the stubble. Piles of them made scratching noises within the wooden beds of the collection wagons in their frantic bid to escape. John felt a bit queasy by the sights and sounds, but Algernon seemed to relish in their hour of desperation.

"The crayfish feast once they have invaded our rice fields, but when we are ready, we harvest them and then feast in return. This is an equitable arrangement, yes? We prefer to regard them as our fresh water lobsters, a cousin to your Maine sea lobsters, I imagine."

John chose not to make a personal comment based upon the uneasy feeling in his stomach; instead, he concentrated and replied as a future scientist. "You have come up with a very practical solution to this infestation problem. You are to be commended for your ingenuity, sir."

Algernon was pleased with the reply. He urged the old horses on, snapping the reins along their backs in an effort to increase their speed, but it was a useless effort. These beasts knew only slow and slower.

"Just up ahead is the rice mill, and next to that, the rice storage barn. Straight ahead, and beyond that levee in the distance, stands our plantation dock and the Mississippi River. We have nearly finished the first quarter of the tour."

"First quarter," repeated John in admiration. "Where can the rest be?"

"Remember, sir, Etenel Babako stretches almost as far as the eye can see. Actually, we have found a way to keep things within their own space, so to speak."

The cart made a left turn and followed the path for about 50 yards around a thick stand of trees and brush. Shortly thereafter, three more outbuildings came into view, but as John was looking at them, he failed to notice that the tree line on his left abruptly ended.

He turned his head to view what had to be hundreds of acres of sugar cane fields. What he thought to be woods was in reality a tree and shrub break that acted as a natural dividing line within the huge plantation.

Algernon pointed and droned on impassively. "The brick building is the sugar mill. The second in line is the boiling house, and the last is the storage barn, where the raw sugar is kept until it is ready for transport to New Orleans for refining. Our mill is powered by oxen, and sometimes horses to a lesser extent."

He smiled. "Both are stronger and more dependable than slaves, although we have been able to train a fair number of our darkies to operate the equipment within the factory and mill, despite their obvious mental deficiencies."

John bit his lip and clenched his teeth hard to keep his anger and thoughts on that subject to himself. His facial expression did not go unnoticed, however, and the overseer had happily discovered a new means with which to stab at him.

"Despite what you might think, young man, our darkies are extremely well treated. As you can plainly see, I carry neither gun nor whip, and the same holds true for the other overseers. I dare say that any random strap marks on their backs are the result of punishments from some prior ownership. We have no need for that HERE, I can wholeheartedly assure you."

John was puzzled; even though he had promised Dr. Pugh to stay clear of the subject, nevertheless he was fascinated. "How, then, do you keep them working, or for that matter, from running off in the faint hope of somehow obtaining their freedom?"

The overseer quickly gave off a hearty, evil laugh. "We have our secret ways at Etenel Babako. It will be the distinct pleasure of Mr.

Dumaine to reveal them to you personally." John was even more puzzled by the reply.

The cart began to wend its way back towards the main house. What seemed like endless rows from the previous year's cane crop sat perched in furrows above drainage ditches laid throughout the confines of the fields. There were also lateral ditches outside of the perimeter.

"Our Louisiana sugar cane craves water, Mr. Larson, but it does not like to take a bath. That is a saying of ours, a little joke."

"Yes, very little," John mumbled quietly. Finally, the cane fields came to an end, and a veritable slew of additional structures came into view. Algernon pointed them out one by one.

"The small wooden buildings straight ahead from left to right are the kitchen, smokehouse, laundry house, and ice house. If you look further to your right, you will see the section designated for the slave quarters. We have a count of 80 darkies at the moment, although one of our females is due to give birth any day now." There was a slight pause; he finished up in a lustful tone and a smile. "She is quite a favorite of mine."

John could not comprehend how people could be treated in such a fashion. While greatly impressed with the plantation, he was thrilled that he and his guide would soon part company, however briefly. The cart pulled up past the kitchen; diagonally to the right was a small wooden residence that was neatly tucked into the rear of the dormant pear tree orchard.

"This house doubles as my home and office," Algernon said proudly. "It is set perfectly between the mansion and the slave shacks. I tend to divide my time between serving Mr. Dumaine's needs and attending to the darkies."

The cart rattled on, finally reaching the rear of the main house as the sun slowly began to set in the west. "Your belongings have been placed in the garconniere, er, guest house. I will take you there."

"That is not necessary," John replied as he stretched his back upward and winced. The work cart was devoid of springs or padded seats for that matter. The ride actually produced nostalgic thoughts of his coach ride to Baltimore. "To be honest, I would very much prefer to walk at this point."

John knew that propriety demanded an acknowledgement for services rendered despite his growing personal dislike for his guide. He would very much have preferred to just walk away without a word; however, he took a deep breath, and let out a short, pre-rehearsed speech.

"Thank you for a very interesting and informative tour, sir. I am sure that you put off other important duties to show me the grounds. I appreciate it very much. Perhaps later in the week I can observe the interior portions of the outbuildings."

"You are quite welcome. I believe it can be arranged." the overseer said blandly with an equal amount of obvious insincerity. They were even.

John began to walk towards the guest house when he stopped in his tracks and turned back towards his reluctant guide. "Excuse me, Algernon. I have been meaning to ask this since I arrived here in Louisiana; just exactly what does Etenel Babako translate to from French into English?"

The overseer's anger rose but quickly subsided; he realized that John meant no disrespect, at least this time. "You are in error, young man. The words Etenel Babako are not French, but actually Cajun."

His composure regained, Algernon cocked his head slightly and snickered, while his dull brown eyes finally shown brightly. "As to its Cajun translation.... it means Eternal Feast; yes, Mr. Larson....Eternal Feast. Dinner is at 8:00PM in the main house. Mr. Dumaine will be expecting you. Good evening."

Chapter 6

An Eventful Evening

After a welcome bath, change of clothes, and a short rest, John stepped out onto the porch of his residence feeling like a new man. The night air had grown cold, even for early April. He put on his coat and began walking to the mansion to meet his host and hopefully have a sumptuous dinner. Although it was dark, he was guided by the brightness of the main house, which had all three floors brightly illuminated in grand style.

As John plodded on towards the lights, he thought he heard a rustling sound a short distance behind him, but every time he stopped to listen, the rustling also ceased. He dismissed the noise entirely, and then quickened his pace towards his impending feast. His stomach was growling noticeably.

When he got to within 50 paces of the main house, something clutched at his right forearm; this caused him to involuntary jerk his body in the opposite direction. He recovered quickly, turned, and braced himself for whatever was to follow. To his great surprise, there stood the old Negro who had brought around the horses and cart for him earlier in the day.

The slave had a look of paternal concern etched on his face, and his eyes were wide with fear. He drew closer and whispered hoarsely while pointing to the mansion; "Take care, yung massah. Dat house be evil. Hear Joshua now. GO HOME!"

Before the startled guest had an opportunity to speak, the old man let out a short moan, released his grip, and slipped back into the darkness. John called out to him in a pleading tone; "Joshua, wait. I need to talk to you...please," but there was no reply. While straining to catch a fleeting glimpse of the old man, John looked off to the west and noticed a number of bon fires dotting the perimeter of the slave quarters. Their area was well lit to be sure. He wondered why.

John completed his walk to the main house with many questions dancing about in his head; as he made his way to the front door, it was opened from the inside by a smallish young Negro woman of about 20 years of age; she was quite attractive. Her black hair was pulled back in a bun that had a short, decorative needle running through it. She wore a modest lime green dress that lacked the familiar frills and puffs so often associated with white Southern women of fashion.

Her complexion was a soft and silky light brown, which only accentuated the delicate features on her face. Her eyes, however, were sad and devoid of that sheen of happiness. She was also very close to giving birth, as evidenced by her protruding stomach. John remembered Algernon's disgusting comment from their plantation tour, and assumed that this was the poor girl to whom he was referring to.

She cast her glance downward and avoided making eye contact whenever possible. "Please come in, sir," she said demurely in very good English. "You are expected."

"Thank you," John replied cheerily. He stepped into the most beautiful entrance hall that he had ever seen. Gleaming cypress floors, partially covered by rich, multi-colored carpets of varying designs drew him into the room. A sparkling glass chandelier hung from the middle of the ceiling, topped off by an intricate, circular white pediment.

Straight ahead on the egg shell white wall was a strangely compelling painting of the stark Louisiana bayous, its dark edges gilded within a golden wooden frame. Directly underneath it was a peach hued, French style sofa with matching square pillows and sheer lace doilies draped over the arms.

The left side of the room featured a curved, mahogany staircase that snaked its way slowly skyward. An ornate, round curved banister of glistening white with matching balusters drew one's eyes magnetically up to the partially hidden, second floor entrance.

Before John could survey the rest of the hall, a melodic voice snapped his train of thought. "Mr. Larson, my name is Mary; if you would follow me, please. Mr. Dumaine has been expecting you."

The young woman closed the front door, spun around and waddled uncomfortably towards the sitting room on the right side of the hall. White, fluted columns announced its entrance way; the room had the option of being made into two by means of long, sliding pocket doors. "Yes," John remarked; "A smoking room for the men, complete with brandy and cigars, and another room for the ladies to enjoy their tea."

A large green vine with red wildflowers dominated the light pink rug that was centered squarely in the room. Plush, rose-colored French couches and chairs were situated throughout. This room's eye catching items were the white marble mantle situated over a wide, deep fireplace, and an immense, beaded glass chandelier with snowflake pediment. Intricate cornice moldings added flair, while several large windows were swaddled in luxurious, sweeping, burgundy draperies.

The woman continued with her pre-set dialogue. "Please be seated, sir. Mr. Dumaine will be with you momentarily. May I get you a refreshment; some wine perhaps, or if you prefer, some cool mint water?

"The mint water will be fine," John replied as he settled into a soft chair in a corner of the room. As she exited quietly, he slowly began to comprehend the grandeur and scale of the entire plantation. The man at the center of such an operation must be an imposing figure indeed, he reasoned. John began to conjure up dramatic images of his host while waiting patiently for his drink; he was quite comfortable.

The sound of heavy, plodding footsteps from the winding staircase announced that the master of the house was approaching. John looked to the entrance of the sitting room. He smiled briefly and thought that if any of his schoolmates would have been with him at this moment, friendly wagers would have been made as to his benefactor's appearance.

After several seconds, John's imagined host came face to face with the real one, and he was greatly disappointed; a fat, balding man of medium height and looking all of 70 rumbled through the doorway. Although he obviously had made an honest attempt to be fairly well-dressed, his clothes were rumpled and did not portray a proper fit by any means. His posture was stooped, and his movements were clumsy, while his brown eyes betrayed the dullness of a man who was not particularly intelligent.

He lumbered in and stuck out his hand in front of John's face before the young man could even rise from his chair. When John got up to shake the man's hand, he noticed two things—the grip, while incredibly strong, was also cold and clammy. John quivered and drew his arm back, wanting to let go immediately.

The old man stared deeply into his guest's eyes, and then released his hold with the slightest bit of contempt that went beyond notice. John had been caught off guard, and his confusion was doubled by trying to decipher any pertinent information from his host's odd handshake.

"I am Jacques Dumaine," he said with the same French style accent as that of Algernon. "Welcome to Etenel Babako, Mr. Larson. I have been awaiting your arrival with great anticipation. I trust your journey has been a pleasant one?"

"As well as could be expected, Mr. Dumaine. Louisiana is quite a beautiful state; and your foreman was kind enough to begin a tour of your plantation this afternoon."

Dumaine frowned. "Algernon is my head overseer, Mr. Larson, not a foreman. We deal with slaves here, not underpaid white laborers, as you do in the North. Negroes require special handling of a kind that I fear you are…unfamiliar with. Algernon is arguably one of the best overseers in the county, and his family has been in my employment for many years. He is quite devoted to me."

Just then, Mary returned with the mint water. She seemed very tense, and gripped the silver tray tightly with both hands while placing it next to John. He opened his mouth to say thank you, but checked himself in time and did not utter a sound, although he did smile and nod to convey his appreciation. This slave business had to be dealt with diplomatically or else he would offend his host. That could result in a very unpleasant nine month stay.

Dumaine watched them both intently, and then summarily dismissed her with a quick command of "Leave us." His low, coarse voice sent a shiver through the young woman, who was all too glad to exit the sitting room.

"She will give birth any day now," he said without emotion. "This will initially result in another mouth to feed for a few years; but, if the child survives, there will be another set of hands to work the fields at a much cheaper price than if he or she were purchased at auction."

John cringed at the heartless line of reasoning, but said nothing to Dumaine, who chuckled at his pained expression. "Come, come, Mr. Larson. Let us dispense with talk of our peculiar institution and move to the dining room. I trust that you have brought your appetite with you? I am very much interested in your plans for increasing my profits by way of, what is the term—crop rotation?"

"Yes, I am a bit hungry, sir," John admitted, "and I will be happy to go over the scientific outline that I have prepared, such as it is."

"Do not be so modest, young man. Dr. Pugh gave quite a glowing evaluation of your capabilities. That is one of the reasons I accepted you in the first place."

The two walked slowly side by side out into the entrance parlor and then the dining room, just off to the left of the staircase. "One of the reasons," John muttered. If Dumaine did not know of him other than from Dr. Pugh's professional opinion, what other reasons could there possibly be?

The dining area brought more architectural delights; an immense, hand carved, oval dinner table made of oak stood ready for use. A robust, dried flower arrangement was nestled comfortably in the table's center, with gold candelabras on either side.

Two padded, high backed wooden chairs sat facing each other at opposite ends of the table, with gleaming, fine china place settings. John thought it strange that he and Dumaine would be sitting so far away from one another, but he shrugged it off to the formalities of Southern propriety.

As soon as they were seated, another female slave entered with their appetizers. Unlike the attractive Mary, this dark, middle aged woman seemed to give off a perpetual scowl on her unflattering face that would make one think twice about issuing her an order despite her lowly status.

She clumsily positioned the plates in front John and Dumaine, and then attempted to make a quick exit. Dumaine remained seated, grabbed her roughly by the forearm, and pulled her to him. He whispered something in her ear as she struggled briefly in fear. When he applied more pressure, she squealed and gave up all pretense of resistance; only then did he release her.

"You may go, Annette," he croaked forcefully. She stiffened, bowed her head slightly, and quietly left the room. John glanced down at his plate to avoid watching the spectacle, but he was pleasantly surprised with what lay before him. "These are Louisiana Gulf shrimp, young man. They are cooked in cane syrup and white wine, along with the requisite assortment of Cajun spices, of course, to form a sweet honey glaze. This happens to be one of my favorite dishes. We Cajuns dearly love our cuisine, and I take great interest in the preparation of ....my food."

"It certainly looks and smells delicious, but please call me John, if you would not mind, sir. It is so much less formal."

Dumaine's eyes gave off a brief shine, as though he had just remembered some amusing story. "As you wish... John," he said in a melodic tone that the young man found unsettling.

"You will be here for quite some time, and I would hope that you will eventually come to consider Etenel Babako as your second home, in a manner of speaking, despite the obvious differences between Louisiana and Pennsylvania." John began to make short work of the shrimp. His host noticed that he was occupied, so he continued on.

"In my case, the Dumaines' and many other Cajun families made their way from Canada via the Mississippi River well over a century ago. This region has become a paradise for us. We would never consider leaving. Now, tell me about your school's theories concerning crop rotation. I am keenly interested in this concept, and hope that you will be able to set up just such a system here at my plantation."

John downed the last of his shrimp, and took a deep drink of mint water before speaking. "Well sir, I understand from your correspondence with Dr. Pugh that your sugar cane crop has shown a decrease in total yield the past few seasons."

"That is all too true," replied Dumaine. "As I am sure you know, sugar cane "ratoons," as we call it, or reemerges from the stubble of the previous year's crop. Our yields have gone down steadily these last 15 years, and Algernon and I are at a loss to reverse this trend."

John wiped his mouth with his soft silk napkin and paused for a moment, recalling the lectures of Professor MacDonald. "The problem, as I see it sir, on a preliminary basis only, you understand, is that the planting of the same crop on a recurring basis has depleted the natural fertilizers in your soil. This in turn will lead to problems with the plant's root system, and a general weakening of the cane itself. I assume that the plants no longer have the height and rich color that they once possessed?"

"That is correct," Dumaine replied, obviously impressed by what he was hearing. "Once upon a time, my cane stood at over 10 feet high. Now, we are happy if we see 8 feet at best. It is most discouraging; also, the actual color of the plants has grown dull."

"If you were to halt cane growing and switch to another crop for several years, sir, you would help to change the soil profile, and also disrupt the life cycles of the insects and pests that infest the cane. This would make those fields undesirable for them to inhabit. Do you follow me?"

"Yes, yes, I do indeed," Dumaine cooed as he leaned forward in his chair, concentrating on John, and digesting what he had just proposed, although he had eaten none of his own dinner.

"Do you believe that you can come up with a suitable alternative planting for a portion of my cane fields to test this theory? Of course, I would not feel comfortable deleting the entire crop in one fell swoop. Etenel Babako is renowned throughout the South for its sugar cane, despite our current problems."

Before John could reply, the main course was brought in by a more civil looking Annette. He glanced hopefully at his plate, only to stare into a heaping dish of what appeared to be some sort of crawfish medley, accompanied by rice.

His stomach turned as he thought of the wriggling mass of muddy crawfish that had been heaped onto the side of the cart path in the rice fields earlier in the day. He took a quick drink of mint water and inhaled slowly while closing his eyes.

"This is crawfish etouffee," Dumaine announced happily, and then droned on, almost like a child reciting the alphabet. "The crawfish are mixed with pepper, onions, Tabasco, flour, mushrooms, butter, garlic…and other ingredients that I cannot recall right now, unfortunately."

John was thrilled with his host's temporary lapse of memory. He came up with a desperate plan that he hoped would keep the main course down and avoid insulting his host. He was well aware that Southerners took great personal pride in their regional dishes. Perhaps he could get through the dinner by shelling some of the crawfish, positioning them on the side of his plate, and then holding his breath while forking them up without actually tasting what was going into his mouth.

It was not much of a plan, but it was all he could come up with on such short notice. There was no dog under the table waiting for scraps like back home in York, and only so many crawfish could be hidden under the rice heap on his plate.

Just as John was about to begin his perfunctory shelling, there was a commotion in the front parlor. Mary came hurriedly into the dining room and announced to Dumaine that a rider had important information for him. He excused himself, and went out into the hallway, where he was met by an excited messenger. John got up from the table to find out what was happening, but his efforts were wasted; Dumaine had ushered the man outside the house.

John heard their excited voices rise, and then intermingle. He could not quite make out what they were saying, but he did recognize the words Charleston Harbor in their brief conversation. Shortly thereafter, Dumaine re-entered the front parlor quite ecstatic, while the sound of horse's hooves trailed off into the distance down main pathway towards the River Road.

"I must beg your pardon, John. I have some urgent business that cannot wait. If you would return to the dining room and finish your meal, Annette will see to you."

Dumaine started for the door, and then stopped. He turned back to John, and spoke with a strange look of evil satisfaction on his face that startled the young man. "Everything is fitting into place exactly as I had hoped for. Very soon, all will be in readiness," he said coldly. "You will begin work tomorrow. Algernon will attend to your needs."

John never did get the chance to reply to his host. Dumaine raced out the door into the night without even closing the door behind him. While he was not quite sure just what had transpired, John had a sense of great relief that he was off the hook for dinner.

He took full advantage of his opportunity and excused himself to both Mary and Annette, claiming that he had numerous preparations to make for the next day's field experiments. He exited the mansion and turned to make his way back to the guest house.

The night air had grown colder still. The two women watched him from a parlor window. Mary had a look of pity, and made a move for the front door, but Annette blocked her path.

"It is none of our business," Annette said emphatically. "There is nothing we can do for him. His fate is sealed."

Mary stood still, lost in her thoughts. After a few moments, she quietly murmured a simple "Yes," and the two returned to their duties.

Chapter 7

Field Studies Begin

John awoke from a deep sleep to a sharp, rhythmical knocking sound. He roused himself from his warm bed and slowly made his way to the front door of the guest house, trying unsuccessfully to shake the cobwebs from his head. He opened the door to find Algernon standing just outside with a pleased look on his face.

The overseer had obviously hoped that he would startle John from his slumber, and he had done so successfully. However, despite his minor victory, his tone was anything but triumphant. "Mr. Dumaine has ordered me to assist you in your crop studies," he said mechanically without much enthusiasm.

"What...What time is it?" John asked weakly.

"It is 6:00AM," Algernon responded; "Your work is to begin now."

John was instantly irritated once again by the overseer's manners and tone, not to mention his choice of words. It was almost as though the brazen Cajun was ordering the young man about like one of the plantation slaves.

"Is it not customary to have BREAKFAST when one gets up in the morning, Mister...Mister...I never did get your last name," John said incredulously.

"I am simply Algernon. Breakfast will be available AFTER you have begun your field assessments."

John's face became flushed with anger. He shut the door unceremoniously in the overseer's face, and methodically put on his work clothes and heavy boots while muttering a slew of oaths under his breath. He bent down and dragged the equipment trunk along the wooden floor with his left hand, and opened the front door with his right. To his surprise, Algernon had not moved an inch; the expression of satisfaction had also remained unchanged.

A large work cart, driven by a big, broad-shouldered Negro pulled up in front. The overseer stepped aside as John pulled the trunk out of the house towards the back of the cart. The slave remained seated, holding the reigns to two of the scrawniest looking mules John had ever seen. Suddenly, Algernon exploded in a rage filled tirade.

"PORTAFOY! PUT THIS TRUNK IN THE CART AT ONCE! HAVE YOU NO EYES?"

The slave dropped the reigns and slowly made his way down off the buckboard. He stepped between both men without a sound, then reached down and took hold of the trunk. He picked it up with little effort, but also made little effort in its handling. The trunk flew unceremoniously into the rear of the cart, while John held his breath, wondering about the condition of his delicate instruments. It would be a cruel joke indeed if they were damaged now that he had arrived at his destination.

Algernon could stand no more. He stepped in front of the slave and the two stood nearly toe to toe. John expected to hear the distinctive smacking sound of the overseer's lash, but he suddenly remembered from the previous day's conversation that the little man carried neither whip nor pistol. Instead, Algernon used the power of language to strike complete subjugation and intense fear into the slave.

"I have had ENOUGH of your INSOLENCE," he bellowed. "Perhaps it is time you received a visit from the MASTER. Yeeees, I think it is high time for a special visit."

The reply to this threat was instantaneous, with the slave clasping his hands together while cringing down in front of his tormentor. "No, no, suh! Portafoy lissen up. No see massah...PLEEEEZ!

Algernon reveled in the poor wretch's terror. He stood stiffly above him grinning broadly, drinking in the abject subservience that he had so quickly inflicted. Finally, he spoke with an air of supreme superiority, awash in a position of power absent of all decent checks or balances.

"You will drive this man wherever he wishes to go, and assist him in any way he desires. You will also keep your mouth shut. Do you understand the directions that I have given to you?" Not waiting for a reply or expecting one, he finished his tongue lashing. "Now...get back in the cart."

He had made his point in heartless, brutal fashion, as he had done so many times before. All that was left was a frightened, groveling heap, a poor soul who was incapable of fighting back. The slave scampered up into the buckboard like an anxious child climbing an apple tree for the first time.

"Yessuuuh. Portafoy take yung' massah roun'. We be fine. We be fine fo' shur."

John was repulsed and embarrassed by the scene he had just witnessed, but also puzzled as to just how the overseer had imposed his will without some form of physical threat. Algernon turned to him and spoke in a low voice so that the Negro could not possibly hear.

"My apologies, sir; a certain female slave on the plantation with whom Portafoy had been smitten was recently sold off by Mr. Dumaine to a nearby plantation owner. This darkie has been quite surly ever since, and I have tried to indulge him, to a point. This will set things right, I assure you."

John's thoughts flew back to Harriet Beecher Stowe's novel, the one that he had read several times. While he had not yet witnessed the book's portrayal of physical brute force, an undeniable sense of hopelessness and despair was evident in the few slaves with whom he had come into contact. He had to continually remind himself of his promise to Dr. Pugh regarding his conduct while at the plantation. Slavery was a festering sore, and a subject to be avoided at all costs.

"Thank you for your help," John said with forced civility as he climbed onto the buckboard. "I will start by taking soil samples from the north cane field furrows, and then run tests from the guest house. I will also need some clean water to insure that the tests are not compromised in any way."

He sat down, winced, and then lifted himself up slightly as he picked a splinter from the seat of his pants. "I should have some preliminary results by tomorrow morning for Mr. Dumaine. We can then devise several action plans to follow up pursuant to the possibility of a crop change." He paused slightly, and then continued on as his voice rose in a questioning tone. "Has he returned from last night's meeting? I do hope that everything is all right?"

John was fishing for information, and Algernon knew it, but the overseer did not take the bait. "Portafoy will provide you with drinking water from the cistern behind the main house. Mr. Dumaine was up all night and is presently...asleep; he left instructions that he is not to be disturbed. Under the circumstances, you may continue with your tests unchecked. As for supper…unless Mr. Dumaine desires your presence, you may take your evening meal alone in the dining hall or the guest house. It is your choice."

John was impressed with the beautiful dining area of Etenel Babako, but the possibility of eating by himself at a formidable table in such a large room would certainly prove lonely and uncomfortable. He chose the latter.

"The guest house will be more sufficient if Mr. Dumaine is unavailable, Algernon, and I will be better able to maximize my studies."

"As you wish," the overseer replied, taking a mental note of what might be the routine for the immediate future. "You will be notified if Mr. Dumaine becomes available to dine with you. As for tomorrow, I will have Portafoy at your door by 6:00AM."

"Make that 7:00AM, if you don't mind," John retorted swiftly. Despite his promise to Dr. Pugh, he was not about to be bullied incessantly by one of Dumaine's employees.

"7:00AM it is, then," Algernon replied with a hint of annoyance and resignation as he began to walk toward his office behind the orchard. "I will be on the plantation at all times if there is anything else that you may require."

He stopped and turned back to John. "And do not interact with the slaves, if you please. They are like ignorant, frightened children, and as such, they are prone to … strange talk. Pay them no mind." He shot a final, wicked glance up at Portafoy and continued on his way.

Portafoy's shoulders tensed up reflexively. He snapped the reins on the old mules sharply, and the cart lurched forward. He looked straight ahead without uttering a sound, knowing full well that Algernon would be keeping a watchful eye on him. After they had driven several hundred yards, the slave relaxed noticeably, but followed the overseer's orders to the letter and remained silent.

The cart pulled up to the outermost cane fields, and then slowed to a halt. John hopped off and went to the rear of the wagon to open the equipment chest. Portafoy got down as well to see if the young man needed assistance.

John took one look at the Negroes huge hands and decided that they were best kept clear of his delicate test tubes and chemicals vials. He cheerfully declined any immediate help, and went about the business of gathering soil samples. He also came to the conclusion that it would be wrong to pepper the silent Portafoy with questions about Dumaine, Algernon, or the appearance of the mysterious visitor from the night before.

This poor slave was in a precarious situation. John did not want to pressure the man into disobeying his overseer, but he secretly hoped that Portafoy might volunteer some information that would shed some light on the odd goings on. That never did occur, although it came to him as no great surprise. The poor man looked quite sad and forlorn all day long; finally, John summoned the courage to ask him the one question that kept playing over and over in his head.

"Portafoy, Algernon mentioned that a woman was recently sold to another plantation. Did you... love her?"

Portafoy looked down to the ground, as though deciding if he should or would reply. Finally, he let out a slow, quiet sigh. "She be my wife; we not's married likes the white folk, but she still be my wife. I knew her from a lil' girl, now she gone foevah, suh."

John was deeply touched by the man's sorrow, but he knew that there was precious little that he could do to rectify the situation. Slave marriages were frowned upon but allowed informally in certain locales. None of them, however, were considered legal or binding in the eyes of the law. Slaves were chattel, and as such, they had no rights whatsoever.

Portafoy and the others were merely private property to be disposed of at the whim of their masters. John could not bring himself to say anything more to his work companion, and he was sincerely sorry that he had opened up a festering wound that would never heal with time. This man was suffering enough. They would continue working for the rest of the day in dual silence.

After obtaining close to 25 samples, interspersed between a hearty breakfast and lunch brought back to the fields by Portafoy, the April sun began its slow descent over the adjacent corn and rice fields. John told his quiet companion that he had obtained all that was necessary for the moment, an announcement that elicited a welcome smile, the only other real interaction that they shared for the day, despite their physical proximity to one another.

Portafoy turned the cart around for the return trip as the sun disappeared from the western horizon. As they left the fields behind and approached the guest house, John could make out the figure of a man pacing swiftly back and forth. It was Algernon. When the wagon got to within a stone's throw of the house, John broke the silence.

"I trust that you have not waited too long, sir," he said in a tone that nearly betrayed his hope for just the opposite. "I was unaware that we were to be back by a prescribed time."

The overseer ignored the false apology; he seemed preoccupied and slightly agitated as he took hold of the lead mule's harness. "Have you gathered what you need for your experiments?" he asked eagerly. "Mr. Dumaine has awakened, and he cannot wait for news. He expects you to report to him this evening."

Now John was the one who became agitated. "I will be able to conduct a number of tests this evening, but each one requires multiple steps, and I have over two dozen samples. I will be able to share some very preliminary findings with Mr. Dumaine later in the evening, hopefully during our DINNER together. I trust that will satisfy his curiosity for the moment. Science cannot be rushed, sir, without opening up a Pandora's Box for mistakes or false hypotheses to escape."

Algernon grinned and seemed struck by the analogy. "You are absolutely right, young man...escape. I will be sure to relay that message to Mr. Dumaine. I do not take it upon myself to speak for him, but I believe that he would be in full agreement with that conclusion."

John watched as the overseer did an about face and made straight for the main house, presumably to update his superior of the day's proceedings. Dumaine seemed right about one thing. Algernon was indeed completely devoted to his superior. John wondered what the strong connection was between the two men.

Portafoy sat motionless on the buckboard with his head down under his wide brimmed hat, trying to remain inconspicuous during the brief conversation. When the overseer left, he got down and took the chest gently off the back of the wagon and brought into the guest house, laying it on a table in the front room.

"Thank you for your assistance today, Portafoy," John said with genuine gratitude. You have been a great help to me. "I hope that we can make further progress tomorrow. I will be ready for you at 7AM."

The Negro started to speak, but abruptly cut himself off. John thought that he had remembered Algernon's orders to keep quiet, so he tried to put him at ease.

"I don't believe that saying goodnight will break any rules. After all, we may be working closely together for some time here. It would be nice if we could become friends, if that is all right with you, of course."

Portafoy looked at the young man, and then turned away as though disgusted with himself. He stopped after opening the door, but did not turn around, finally uttering his first words since the early morning hours. They were as fervent as any prayer John had heard during church services back home in York.

"Pleez Lawd, bless yung' massah's soul dis night. He be needin' help, fo' shur." The door closed softly, leaving John alone to ponder the words and actions of his reluctant companion.

Chapter 8

A Creature Attacks

John looked absently at his silver pocket watch as he sat at his work table amidst tubes, books, mounds of dirt, and vials of chemicals. He had been conducting tests in his room and had completely lost track of the time. Willie, the little house slave, had brought an 8PM dinner invitation from Mr. Dumaine just as he had settled down to his work in the guest house. John certainly did not want to offend his host by being late.

He sprang from his chair and put on his coat and boots. Gathering notes that he had made for the last several hours, he rushed from the cottage, walking diagonally towards the path that led to the main house. John still had close to 10 minutes to spare.

The night air was crisp, cool, and clear. Off to his right in the distance, he could make out the unmistakable glow and sputter of the large bonfires that he now surmised habitually dotted the slave quarters, yet he saw no one milling about outside of the cabins or even the grounds for that matter.

John wondered why the slaves would be trying their best to keep the night at bay. They certainly could not be worried about wild animals here. He chalked it up to native superstitions that had possibly been handed down to them from their ancestors in Africa, or some other distant locations from which they had been unmercifully snatched.

There was no Joshua imploring John to leave while on his walk to the mansion this night. He arrived at the front of the house, with Mary once again waiting in the open doorway. John gave a cheerful "Good evening," but she muttered an unintelligible reply and kept her focus on the floor. Once inside the sitting area, he was met by an anxious Dumaine, who strode out of the dining room so quickly that John was taken aback by the old man's speed.

"Well, young man, I see that you have brought some information for me, yes?"

"That is correct, sir, although I must preface my remarks by stating that this data is preliminary in nature, and therefore subject to change pending further research."

"Of course, of course," he replied quickly. "But I have forgotten my duties as host. Please step into the dining room, where we can discuss this more comfortably over dinner."

The two made their way into the dining room, and took their respective places at opposite ends of the table. John gave a brief outline of his day in the fields over shrimp cocktail and a dry, white wine. He was famished, and hoped that the appetizer was an encouraging sign for the main course. The thought of the previous night's crawfish brought on some initial queasiness to his stomach.

He was certain that if the fare was not to his liking this evening he would not have the benefit of an interrupted dinner. While the still sullen looking Annette removed the first course plates, albeit carefully, Dumaine pressed John for information on the condition of his cane fields.

"John, please tell me about the status of the cane soil, and what can be done about it. It is of the greatest concern to me."

John leafed through his notes until he came to the page that he was looking for. "The way I see it, sir, based on my calculations, is that the cane has required the same nutrients year after year, to the point where the soil has become nearly depleted. The ratoons are also showing signs of root damage, and the effects of several sequential seasons of temperatures below 62 degrees Fahrenheit. If things were to continue on this course, you can expect your last cane crop in about....ah....five years or so."

Dumaine was startled by the abruptness of the findings, and he did not mask his uneasiness. "Are hundreds of my acres to be lost forever? What can you do to prevent such a catastrophe?"

Just then, Annette entered with the main course, which was placed gingerly on the table. John was afraid to look, but he was buoyed by Dumaine's announcement. "Ah, chicken and sausage gumbo over rice; I hope you have brought your appetite tonight."

John and his stomach were quite relieved. He forked into the gumbo lustily, and answered the question put before him by his nervous host.

"I would recommend a crop rotation of your present cane fields over a three year period, beginning with the upcoming planting season. For this spring, I would take one third of the fields and convert them to the growing of sweet potatoes. Next year, I would take another third and covert the acres to soybeans. For the last year, I would switch to tomatoes. This is, of course, based upon what amendments can be incorporated quickly into the depleted soil."

Dumaine stared at his guest intently. "And do you have the knowledge and enough equipment from the college at your disposal to insure that this can be accomplished with a fair degree of success?"

"Yes, sir; that is why I am here, to advance the crop rotation theory. I will be at your disposal until the initial crop of sweet potatoes is harvested."

John's affirmation was music to Dumaine's ears. He put down his knife and fork, which he had been using to play with his food, and settled back comfortably into his chair, placing his hands on the front edges of the arm rests.

"I must admit that you are a bright young man, even if you are.....a YANKEE. I can see why the college selected you." John was stung by the boldness of his host, and he felt from the tone of the man's voice when he uttered the word Yankee that Dumaine was no friend of the North.

"What do you make of the recent secession of Louisiana and other southern states from the Union, John? Do you and your kind feel threatened?" John tried to suppress his anger for the sake of Dr. Pugh, but he was having great difficulty. He raised his voice to just below that of a shout.

"I must respectfully remind you that I am not one of your house servants, Mr. Dumaine, and MY KIND will not allow the solidarity of the United States to be threatened by the likes of fire eaters and slave mongers. The republic will be preserved at all costs, come what may!"

"You must pardon my drift into political matters, young man," Dumaine replied without much enthusiasm, "and my poor choice of words. It was not my intention to offend you, particularly when you are here to help."

The rest of the evening's conversation touched upon matters that would cause no offense to either end of the table. Finally, the old man made a somewhat abrupt announcement, as though he had come to a decision of some magnitude.

"If you would excuse me once again, John, I have some pressing household matters that need immediate attention. I know that we have yet to sample brandy and cigars together, but there will be plenty of time for that. I beg your indulgence. Goodnight." Dumaine placed his napkin on the food of the plate in front of him, shot his guest a quick, expressionless look, and exited the room.

Still stung by the earlier verbal joust with Dumaine, John was thrilled to be out of the old man's presence. He purposely sat and waited for several minutes, hoping to put some distance between himself and his host, then gathered his notes and left the mansion behind with nary a nod to the house slaves.

As he began his walk back to the guest cottage, John could not believe what had just taken place. Despite the forced civility, he was certain that there was some form of animosity and anticipation stirring within Mr. Dumaine towards him; but why he did not know. Now he was possibly on bad terms with the plantation's chief overseer AND the owner! How could things have spiraled out of control so fast, and with so little warning?

This could prove to be a very long stay. And to top it all off, he never got the opportunity for the brandy and cigars. When John arrived back at the guest house, his eye caught sight of a small cross tacked up over the front door. He reached up and gently pulled it down. Once inside, he brought it over to the hurricane lamp by his work table for a closer inspection.

He scratched his index finger against the side of the cross, and determined that the material was a hardened, red, clay-like substance.

There was also Spanish moss, bright colored feathers, and the same type of mountain ash and hawthorne twigs offered by the old woman in New Orleans tied onto the cross with some hemp.

He did not understand the sudden appearance of this cross, but he was fairly confident from the composite materials that it reflected some aspect of Voodoo worship. This led him to believe that one of the plantation slaves had placed it over the door, but the more important question was…for what purpose? Was the placement designed to help or hurt him? He had done nothing to get singled out for their black magic mumbo jumbo.

He thought back to his previous evening's encounter with Joshua, and then shrugged the cross off to a well meaning but ignorant old man's superstitions. But why would Joshua believe that he was in need of protection, or say that Dumaine's house was evil? If John was to be working on the plantation for the foreseeable future, it might be best to find out sooner rather than later.

After depositing his notes inside, he started in the direction of the slave quarters, quietly passing the overseer's office, and headed towards the eastern most section of the property. As he grew closer to the triple row of one room shacks, his initial observations were confirmed.

While there were large fires situated throughout the perimeter and main pathways, he could not see any slaves walking about. John thought this quite odd, considering the fact that Algernon had mentioned he had control over 80 Negroes. Could every last one of them be indoors? He took out his watch; it was nearly 10PM; the children and old ones would be asleep, but some adults should still be awake and up and around.

John reached the first line of poorly constructed, pine clapboard shacks. Each one had a raised porch covered by an extended roof of bark strips. Every door was closed, and every window was shuttered. Silence reigned, save for the crackle of the fires. Gray smoke from crude chimneys rose in unison towards the night sky; this was the only clue that there were in fact people inside.

He completed his solitary walk passed the first long row of shacks and stopped at the end when he reached several large privies. Turning around quickly to evade the unmistakable smell, he worked his way back along the middle row, which was eerily similar to the first. What unnerved him the most, upon a closer inspection, were tiny crosses placed over each doorsill and window; they were a smaller version of the one he had discovered at the guest house. John decided to find Joshua and put an end to the mystery.

Summoning up his courage, he stepped up onto the porch of the last hut in the row and knocked on the front door. The muffled cries of women and children followed immediately. When the door did not open, he raised his voice and asked where he could find Joshua. This was met with wailing from several adjacent huts, but still no replies, and no answers.

John thought it best not to impose on any of the people inside; he would wait until morning before renewing his investigation. The slaves were too frightened to be of any help at the moment. Perhaps in the light of day he could coax some information out of Portafoy, or even chance upon Joshua in the fields.

Besides, he was getting tired. John made his way back slowly to the guest house, and threw himself onto the bed. It was then that he felt the clay cross in his back pocket. It had broken into pieces. He got up, reached back and took them out, piling the contents on the seat of a nearby chair.

At that same moment, John heard a distinct knock. Who would be calling on him here, at this hour? He reached for the slide bolt to unlock the door, and cracked it open slightly to catch a peek of who was waiting outside. To his amazement, it was Jacques Dumaine. His voice was soft and contrite.

"I am sorry to interrupt you at this late hour, young man, but I wonder if I could have a word with you about our dinner conversation earlier this evening. There is something that I must explain to you. May I enter?"

John was thrilled at this golden opportunity to set things right with his host, who seemed to be extending the olive branch of peace. Apologies would be tendered by both sides to save face, and the unpleasant politics that sparked this brushfire would be avoided at all times in the future. "Of course, Mr. Dumaine; I am most anxious to speak with you. Please do come in."

Not one second after the words had left his lips; the door was ripped from its hinges and thrown inside up against the back wall. Dumaine strode in triumphantly with eyes akin to blazing embers, his face contorted in a macabre look of maniacal rage, hate, and bloodlust. John froze on the spot, unable to move or utter a sound.

Dumaine grabbed him roughly by the throat with both hands and throttled him like a dog would a downed squirrel. "I am here to finish our dinner conversation," the old man began with a grimacing smile as John gasped desperately for air.

"You shall stay far beyond this planting season, my young friend. I have need of your knowledge and expertise. When you awaken, you will begin to learn what it is you have become, and what it is you are to do."

Dumaine hurled John to the floor with a dull thud, and then straddled above his helpless, startled prey in supreme triumph. He slowly got down on his knees, took hold of the young man's hair, and jerked the head violently to one side. The old man bent over and opened his mouth wide, exposing gleaming wide incisors before tearing into the exposed neck. John was finally able to let out a single, futile scream for help before he blacked out, but it only served to heighten Dumaine's moment of pleasure.

Hundreds of miles away, blissfully unaware that the student they sent south was being savaged at that very moment, Dr. Pugh and Professor MacDonald were standing on the front steps of the Old Main building discussing the recent turn of national events.

"I still cannot bring myself to believe that it has actually come to this, Mac. Our country is being torn asunder; we are at war!"

"You had best believe it, Evan, and in a hurry," MacDonald said dejectedly. "The President has called upon the governors of all states and territories still loyal to the Union for 75,000 volunteers to stamp out this rebellion. Our standing army boasts of no more than 17,000 regular officers and enlisted men, and no one can be sure of their sympathies."

"What do you mean? These are United States soldiers!"

"I mean that all men must soon decide where their true loyalties lay, Evan, either with their own individual states, or with the Republic. There are Southerners in the ranks, including many fine officers trained in the art of war at our own Military Academy at West Point."

"Mac, those officers have all sworn an oath to defend the flag. They dare not take up arms against it. It is blasphemy and…and…treason! Yes, treason, by God!"

"Treason or no, good men will resign with heavy hearts and head south. I have no doubt that Lincoln's call for armed troops to defeat the Rebels will strike a patriotic cord. The quota will surely be met."

MacDonald continued, "But, on the other hand, how many Southern men with Union loyalties will bolt passed the Mason Dixon Line if they perceive the President's proclamation as a threat aimed directly at their homes and loved ones? What are they to do?"

"I thank the Lord that I personally am in no such position," Dr. Pugh replied weakly, "although I fear that we will lose students to both armies, if it truly comes to armed conflict."

MacDonald looked at his friend with sadness and anxiety. "Are you not forgetting someone, my dear Evan?"

"Of course not," Pugh snapped back, noticeably hurt by the insinuation. "Young Larson has been on my mind constantly since the fall of Sumter. But he is no soldier, merely a student. I cannot believe that the proper authorities in Louisiana would bother him in any way, shape, or form."

Dr. Pugh paused for a moment for reassurance from MacDonald, but to his great surprise, he did not receive it. This made him even more agitated, and his voice rose in fear. He suddenly began to pace back and forth while wringing his hands.

"His purpose there is purely a scientific one. A blind man could see that he is no spy. Jacques Dumaine is a proper gentleman, and he will see to the boy's welfare, I am certain."

MacDonald tried to calm his colleague. "Evan, I have always trusted in your judgment. If you feel that John is not in harm's way, then I will not send him this." He held up an envelope.

"What have you there?" Pugh asked.

"It is a letter to John advising him to abandon his experiments and return to the Agricultural College immediately. However, I know that you would never compromise the safety of any of the young men left in our care, so I will put it aside and wait for his correspondence to arrive."

"Thank you for your trust, Mac, AND your friendship," Pugh sighed. "I am sure that this entire affair will be over in a few months. Cooler heads will prevail, you shall see. I have great faith in our elected officials. I'll wager that young Larson is sleeping like a baby as we speak."

While John's life blood was being furiously sucked out of him, Marie Laveau sat in a darkened corner of the French Quarter's St. Louis Cathedral, rhythmically swaying back and forth, moaning in sorrow. After a brief respite, she rose, exited the pew, and slowly made her way to the world outside. The warm night air brushed her tear stained face as she opened the massive wooden door. By the time she reached the bottom of the stairs, the essence of John Larson was gone forever.

Chapter 9

Death and Submission

John was lying face up on the floor of the guest house when he finally returned to consciousness. Staring up at the ceiling, he strained his eyes and blinked repeatedly until his vision had regained its focus. He rose tentatively, shuffled over to the edge of the bed, then sat down and slumped over, totally spent. After several minutes, he looked slowly around the room. The shattered front door had been repaired, put back on its hinges, and closed shut; but even stranger was the fact that the windows were now boarded up from the inside.

John stood up, staggered towards the work table, and fell to one knee. As he struggled to regain his equilibrium, he noticed a small pool of what looked like dried blood on the floor in the middle of the room. The memory of the horrifying episode with Dumaine came roaring back like a flood through a breached earthen dam. He instinctively grabbed for his neck, and then winced in pain as his hand touched the spot that the crazed old man had savaged.

He raced to the door and flung it open, determined to find a safe refuge for the rest of the night, and then make his escape on the Mississippi in the early morning. There would certainly be a paddle wheeler or cotton barge passing near the plantation's loading dock. He would flag it down and put as much space as possible between himself and the obviously demented Jacques Dumaine.

John wasn't sure if the local authorities would believe such a bizarre story, particularly from an outsider. He almost didn't care, just so long as he was as far from the plantation as possible and heading home. John felt a strange chill throughout his body, but he assumed that was as a result of the loss of blood from the attack; just how much blood he had no way of knowing.

He was shocked to discover that dusk had just begun to settle in. That could mean only one thing--he had been unconscious for nearly a full day; that would explain the time needed to repair and reinforce the guest house. This fact that should have added to his bewilderment; and yet, the coming twilight seemed to have a calming effect on his thoughts, while his raging desire for escape slowly began to ebb.

John's terror had also slackened noticeably. Instead of running from Dumaine, he now wanted to seek out his strange host, although he could not quite understand why. The mansion seemed the logical choice to start. He had never actually seen the old man anywhere else on the plantation.

While making his way towards the main house, John stumbled upon two Negroes scurrying to lock up the barn and stable for the evening. They yelped in surprise and stopped dead in their tracks, crossing themselves repeatedly in a terrified frenzy. In a few moments, they made a mad dash for the slave quarters, which by now had its perimeter fires burning brightly.

John's eyes followed them intently with a hunger that he could not explain; without so much as a second thought, he was in hot pursuit. The Negroes began screaming frantically for fellow slaves in their tiny village to let them inside the shacks. John closed in just as they reached the encampment; doors to several adjoining hovels cracked open ever so slightly. One slave jumped onto a porch and burst through the unlocked door, after which it was summarily slammed shut.

The other Negro was not so fortunate. He tripped in a cart rut just a few feet from safety and tumbled to the ground on his side. Knowing full well that his pursuer was close behind, the wretch turned over on his back, and clutched at an odd looking necklace that was slung loosely around his neck.

John's bloodlust was up; he snarled furiously and flung himself at the prostrate form, only to be hurled backwards by the most horrific smell that he had even encountered. The Negro wailed in fear and tore off the necklace, then held it out stiffly in front of him. John was furious with this new development, and he bore down once more on his prey, smell be damned.

Just as he was about to pounce, doors opened up and down along the long row of shacks; slaves young and old darted out and took aim, hurling fists and pots full of garlic in John's direction. He suddenly swooned, thrashed his arms about wildly, and then grabbed at his stomach, gagging violently to the point of vomiting and passing out altogether.

While John remained temporarily disoriented, the fallen stable slave took full advantage of his opportunity; he sprang up and darted through the closest open door, which was once again slammed shut immediately behind him. John lurched forward, only to be pelted with more garlic as he staggered along the slave quarters long corridor. This was a fight that he could not win, and one that he could not understand. Why was he so strongly repelled by the smell of something as innocent as common garlic? But of even greater importance, why did he have the urge to rip at the throats of the Negroes in order to quell his intense feeling of hunger?

His rational mind understood that his actions were bizarre and unspeakable, yet his feelings relayed a much different story, one that kept echoing a reassuring theme--this was a very natural thing to do. He decided to follow up on those feelings, although deep down, he somehow knew that there was little choice in the matter.

The first order of business was to escape the suffocating atmosphere of the garlic. John's intention was to run as fast as his legs could carry him, but to his great surprise, he found himself literally catapulted into the air, high above the shacks and the wafting stench. As he spread his arms and hovered above the tree line, his head cleared in the cool, dry air; the only smell that he encountered now was the burning oak fires pock marked throughout the slave encampment.

John knew that he was now safe from immediate harm, but that did nothing to quell the gnawing hunger that was growing steadily inside him. He spent the next several hours gliding over the outbuildings and grounds in a foggy, surreal state, waiting impatiently for any sign of movement in the darkness. Eventually, he found the sensation of flying to be as natural as walking, and he soon discovered that his senses had increased exponentially, particularly those of sight and sound.

While trolling near the mansion, he finally spied something moving at a leisurely pace through the west bowling green and into the adjoining apple orchard. John darted straight for it. As he got closer, he discerned that it was a plow horse, one that had probably gotten loose from the open stable that the two slaves had never gotten the opportunity to properly secure.

The horse stopped abruptly in mid stride; it sniffed the air, snorted briefly, and cocked its head from one side to the other. The animal sensed danger was approaching, but could neither see nor hear anything of consequence. It pawed at the ground anxiously, and then whinnied in fear and pain as John landed hard onto its back, grabbed its mane, and plunged his mouth into the horse's strong, ample neck.

The poor horse reared, bucked, and spun around repeatedly, but there was no way to shake off this hellish rider. John ripped and sucked away long and hard; soon the horse's front legs dropped to the ground, then it keeled slowly over onto its side and flailed with all four hooves in a final, futile effort.

When it was all over, John stood up, dusted himself off, and wiped his mouth. He looked at the smeared blood on his hands with fascination, and rubbed some between his thumb and forefinger. For some reason, he was only partially sated despite the large amount of blood that he had just ingested.

Then it struck him that animals should only be consumed under the direst of circumstances. He ultimately required human blood; he had run out of time, however. But how and why had those thoughts entered his head? The dawn was fast approaching, and something deep inside beckoned him to return to the guest house immediately; it was his own sense of self preservation.

There was no time for further reflection on these matters; he flew to his dwelling and obligingly closed and locked the door behind him. He was tired and confused. There was so much to think about, so much to discover, and so much to learn. John knew that there was only one person who could adequately answer all of his questions

As he lay down in his bed and covered himself from head to toe with a thick woolen blanket, he was certain that his next destination must be the plantation house. That was his last thought before sleep, and his first thought upon rising the following evening. He opened the door to a beautiful dusk, and made his way once again along the path to the mansion.

Jacques Dumaine was bobbing slowly back and forth in his favorite rocking chair on the second floor balcony, awaiting his new disciple's arrival. When John turned the corner of the house and reached the front pillars, the old man called down to him.

"You have come at last, my friend. A beautiful evening, don't you think? The darkness always renews one's strength, and never fails to sooth a restless spirit. How do you feel?"

John looked up. "My God, what have you done to me?"

Dumaine was amused yet stung by the question. He quickly bound over the railing and landed effortlessly on the ground below. "God has nothing to do with this, although I dare say that by our very existence, He has given at least tacit approval. But enough unpleasant talk of the deity. You have come to find out what it is you are, and what I have planned for you, yes?"

"I already begin to realize what I am," John replied with some small measure of disgust.

"Good. The negative feelings will pass in a matter of days, I can assure you. There is yet some humanity left in you, but once you begin to feed on a regular basis, that will dissipate, along with all resistance to the...transformation."

Dumaine paused. "But I sense that you already know that. Your real interests lie in the future, or more accurately, YOUR future, am I not correct?" John did not answer, but nodded slowly in agreement.

"As I mentioned previously, I have an extensive, or shall I say, a long term need of your expertise; hence, your present condition. In order to reverse the decline of the soil for ALL of my cane fields, as you have recommended, I had to make sure that you will remain here for an indeterminate number of years. The reversal will be a very time consuming process, as you yourself have previously pointed out."

Dumaine stopped for a moment to see if there were any objections to that conclusion. He received none, and continued. "I expect you to return all designated acreage to sugar cane production as soon as your soil depletion tests are more favorable. Sugar cane has made Etenel Babako famous in the past, and it will do so again in the future."

"Finally, I dare say that if your crop rotation theory is correct, and I am sure that it is, the current problems with my cane will also manifest themselves in the remaining acreage on the plantation, which has begun to show slightly lower yields after many years of continuous plantings of corn and rice. You will oversee the substitution for those crops as well."

Oddly enough, John considered Dumaine's reasoning to be thoroughly sound, from both a practical and scientific point of view. He also knew that he should have been feeling outrage and a sense of violation for all of this being forced upon him, but there was only emptiness. Dumaine chimed in on his thoughts.

"As I mentioned, a great deal of your human emotions have been drained from your body... along with your blood, of course; although I daresay that while the transformation gradually takes place, certain predatory instincts will manifest themselves quite readily."

But there was something in Dumaine's explanations that did not quite fit, and John needed to know why. "If, as you say, my humanity will disappear entirely, why then do YOU continue to care for this plantation with such a....passion?"

Dumaine hesitated, as though he were caught off guard, but he answered the question straight out. "That is a very keen observation AND choice of words, my young apprentice. You are to be congratulated; but have no doubts; you WILL lose your humanity. However, you shall keep just one shred of it, nonetheless." John inched closer to him as he spoke. The scene was not unlike that of a young boy listening attentively to the sage advice of his aged grandfather.

"This lone vestige may be in the form of a person, an object, or even an idea, but it will have been the most important thing in your past life, and it will stay with you forever. This "passion," as you call it, is different for each of our kind. In my own case, it was and will always be my love for Etenel Babako."

John's mind raced quickly passed friends, family, the college, even hometown York; there was no feeling, but also no pain. "I can't think of anything like that for myself. Is that wrong, Dumaine?"

"No, it only means that you do not yet realize what it is that you cherished most in life. The answer may come next week, next year, or in 100 years. You will have an eternity to find THAT out."

While John pondered his new situation, Dumaine gave it structure. "John Larson, as the one who has brought about your transformation, you are bound to me. With that, I charge you to remain on this plantation until the work I desire has been completed. Once that has taken place, you shall be free to go where you will. Only the discovery of your one true passion can alter the terms of this servitude. Do you understand your situation as I have explained it?"

There was an awkward silence as the two night creatures eyed each other intently. "That I do," John replied with mixed feelings of resignation and acceptance. "I WILL fulfill my obligations, you may rest assured; but....what of my parents, and of Dr. Pugh and Professor

MacDonald? Will they not become suspicious when I do not return as scheduled for the new school term?"

Dumaine answered matter-of-factly. "You will write to all of them regularly as though nothing has happened. Come early October, make it perfectly clear that it is imperative you continue your crop rotation studies here at the plantation for another full growing season. I am sure that you can devise some reasons for this change in plans?"

John thought for a moment. "Most certainly; there is the monitoring of winter temperatures and water saturation levels in the soil, along with checking for various insect infestations. Yes, that should be more than enough reasons to warrant an extended stay here; and the college would be thrilled with the additional cold season data that the other four students would not be in a position to provide. As for my parents, timely letters will keep them satisfied."

"Excellent," responded Dumaine. "I see that I have indeed chosen wisely. You have already commenced with the changeover. That is good; but I am sure that by now you must be hungry. Dumaine moved closer and continued speaking, this time with controlled anger, although it was not directed at John. "You were correct in your assumption that it was Joshua who placed that abomination on the guest house door to thwart my plans. I will not tolerate resistance in any shape or form. That is one of the many pleasures of absolute power. Algernon has given him the late day task of mucking some stalls in the stable. You will find him there now. Go and drink deeply."

"But…once he is dead, will Joshua not then become one of…us?

Dumaine raised his eyebrows, and his face drew tight with the importance of the information he was to impart on his new pupil. "You are not to drain him completely. When you are done feasting, Algernon will give him final ....attention, so to speak. You will require sustenance several times per week. Make sure that you do not kill your prey, or they will most assuredly become like us."

"By prey you mean the slaves," John remarked.

"ABSOLUTELY NOT," Dumaine spewed with marked irritation. "They are much too valuable a commodity to waste on mere feasting! Food may be obtained quite readily in Baton Rouge, and even more so in New Orleans. Prostitutes, thieves, charlatans, and drunkards are rarely missed from the general populace."

Dumaine went on. "Even lawyers may be chosen, depending on their character, or lack of it. I shall bring them back to you as needed; Algernon will finish them off upon the conclusion of your meal. Afterwards, the carcasses will be gutted and cast into the muddy Mississippi; the river is an excellent dumping site that rarely gives up its secrets."

John was mesmerized by the information provided by his host turned murderer and now mentor. "You seem to have thought of everything, Dumaine. Etenel Babako is appropriately named. This plantation can most certainly provide an eternal feast, if it is properly administered, and OUR numbers kept in check to avoid detection."

"Quite so; we are perfectly safe here, away from prying eyes, loose tongues, and those knowledgeable few who would relish in our destruction. Now attend to your dinner, then meet me back at the library. There is still much to discuss about to your new...situation, and how you are to properly explain and coordinate the continued field experiments with Algernon relative to your new daylight restrictions."

John looked doubtful for the first time, but Dumaine understood, and made an effort to quell his misgivings. "Algernon will be of invaluable service to you, as he is to me. There WAS some initial resentment on his part concerning your arrival. As head overseer on the plantation, he takes his duties quite seriously. He felt that he could reverse the decline of the cane crop without outside interference, so naturally, he regarded your arrival as a personal affront."

Dumaine smiled. "However, now that your own situation has changed, he will give you due deference and be as pliant as a lapdog, but without the fleas…I believe."

John was relieved that there would be no further verbal jousting with the overseer. As he made his way towards the barn, he experienced the additional waves of gnawing hunger that Dumaine knew would manifest. His mind recalled that Joshua recently risked his own life to warn him, a stranger, of the dangers lurking about.

That should have generated a reciprocal response on John's part; but there were no feelings of gratitude, pity, or remorse when he ravenously drained the blood from the pleading old Negro with hardly a struggle. His strength had increased tenfold to go along with his "renewal," courtesy of Dumaine, and he enjoyed it immensely.

Algernon was sitting patiently on the top rail of the corral fence when Louisiana's newest night creature staggered from the barn with the strangest mixture of satisfaction and horror etched on his face. John was attempting to come to grips with the fact that not only had he nearly sucked the very life out of a human being, but also that the act in and of itself was totally exhilarating.

His mind was swimming with conflicting thoughts and emotions. The transformation was continuing to take place rapidly, just as Dumaine had promised. He stopped by the corral gate and looked over at Algernon, who was enjoying the obvious inner turmoil immensely.

"Do not think too badly of yourself, my new master. Soon, this will all feel quite natural. In fact, you will hardly feel anything at all."

A pitiable groan came from just inside the stable, prompting the overseer to hop off and make his way to the barn door. Joshua was attempting to get to his feet in a final bid for escape, but the old man was too far gone for physical exertion of any kind. He dropped face down in a heap onto a hay bale and lay there like a half shredded scarecrow.

"Oh Lawd," he pleaded faintly, "pleez gives Joshua da strength."

Algernon smiled and raised a shovel high in the air as he drew closer to the helpless slave. "The Lord helps those who help themselves, you fool." He battered the poor Negro with four direct blows to the head, accentuating each direct hit with a word. "Is....that....not....so?"

Joshua's life was over, but so too was the pain, suffering, degradation, and constant fear. Algernon flipped him over, then took out a long knife that was tucked under his waistband. With one quick thrust, the blade penetrated the body deeply just below the naval, and continued upwards to the breast bone.

"No need to see you resurface later; that would be about as close to a resurrection as you could ever hope for, darkie." The overseer took the body in his arms and carried it to his waiting horse. He tied one end of a rope around the old man's neck, then mounted his horse and tied the other end around the saddle horn.

"Let the parade begin," he announced triumphantly to John, who watched impassively. "The slaves must be constantly reminded who is in charge, and what the punishment is for deceit against the Master."

John surmised Algernon's next destination. There was no further need to provide this sadist with an audience, so he turned away with a tinge of disgust and walked towards the lights of the mansion. Dumaine was waiting in the library to further explain this bizarre but exciting new world to him.

Algernon slowly steered the horse with Joshua dragging behind to the long rows of shacks that were the slave quarters. The remains of the old man were now completely covered with dirt; his intestines burst forth from his gutted stomach, and his neck was bent and compressed by the noose. Occasionally, the body would hit a large stone on the ground and seem to jump with life for a split second.

"COME OUT!" Algernon bellowed. "Come out and see what becomes of all those who betray the Master's love with treachery."

Doors and windows opened ever so slightly, just enough for all to get a glimpse of the smirking overseer with the beloved old man in tow. Algernon thought it odd that there were no outward displays of grief or emotion from the group, but then again, they were only miserable slaves, and not worth the effort. Little did he realize that as he made his way towards the Mississippi to dispose of Joshua's body, the twin sisters of Rage and Revenge were now seething behind those closed doors, just waiting for the right moment to strike.

Chapter 10

A Sinister Switch

Dumaine proved to be entirely correct. In the coming days and weeks, the many slender threads of humanity that John retained after the attack slowly thinned out and disappeared from his consciousness. He retained all of his past knowledge and experiences, but there was no emotion attached to them, and he did not suffer the loss.

His feelings were replaced by instinctual drives---hunger, survival, and the thrill of the kill. Twilight became the signal for his awakening, while lingering at dawn caused him great pain, characterized by an intense and excruciating body heat that necessitated an immediate return to the cool, dark safety of the shuttered guest house.

The experiments in selected portions of the cane fields resulted in a subsequent spring changeover to sweet potatoes, coordinated by John and implemented by the steady hand of Algernon, who did in fact prove quite useful after all.

As per Dumaine's plan, John sent regular written reports to Professor MacDonald pursuant to the status of the crop rotation, along with personal correspondence to Dr. Pugh, some ex schoolmates, and of course, his parents. There was nothing tangible in those letters to anyone to indicate that the John Larson they knew and loved was gone forever.

John did find it strange that return letters were few and far between, but he did not dwell on that for very long; his attention was centered upon his new powers and sense of immortality, not on the actions or feelings of mere mortals. Little did he know that his host had been intercepting any mail from Pennsylvania, carefully reading through it, and subsequently discarding whatever correspondence he thought might prove to be a disruption to the new routine at Etenel Babako.

John soon understood Dumaine's assessment that human beings were merely for sport and feasting, and he pledged that he would faithfully follow the old night creature's modus operandi that only the dregs of society should be singled out. No one would waste time searching in an official capacity for the kind of rabble that Dumaine brought back to John for his nourishment.

Although John was rarely afforded the opportunity to choose his own prey, since he was bound to the plantation by Dumaine's edict, he was never disappointed with the selection from the new menu. However, he was able to hone his hunting skills on whatever live game was brought back by his mentor, just as long as the two legged prey remained on the grounds proper.

Occasionally, to his good fortune, he would discover a disoriented runaway slave from a nearby plantation, or some weary vagabond come in off the River Road looking for a night's shelter. But when all was said and done, he particularly enjoyed tracking down the occasional black hearted lawyer brought back by Dumaine from New Orleans.

That certainly brought the most satisfaction; the wild eyed fools, upon becoming totally exhausted from the chase, would invariably attempt to negotiate their way out of death as though pleading a case before a rabid judge. Of course, the final sentence was always the same.

Time passed rather quickly, and October brought with it John's carefully worded request to the Agricultural College for an additional year's stay at Etenel Babako. After several tense weeks of waiting,

Dumaine informed John that he had received the official letter from Dr. Pugh giving his wholehearted approval. It was a moment of great relief to both of them. There had been no firm backup plan to insure John's stay if Dr. Pugh had not given his blessing to the extension. Everything was moving along splendidly.

As long as he kept up appearances by way of regular reports and personal letters, John would remain safe at the plantation. He discovered that he reveled in the safety and security that Dumaine had provided, and he gratefully returned the favor to his temporary master by formulating the expanded crop rotation plans with the timely assistance of Algernon. The overseer kept the slaves cooperative and productive via the continuous threat of face to face meetings with Dumaine and now John.

In the late fall, the remaining acreage of sugar cane was prepared for the changeover, based upon favorable soil tests of the previously converted front fields; weakened ratoons were removed, while the furrows were lowered. This late season work would furnish Algernon with more time to devote to the spring planting of sweet potatoes.

Part of John's first winter season at the plantation was spent in the monitoring of the fluctuating Louisiana temperatures. A hard winter would keep the insect pest population in check. His inspections of the water saturation levels in the soil also indicated that the man made levees along the river needed to be reinforced, a backbreaking task, but Algernon lorded over the helpless Negroes with foul delight.

John's routine of night time activities centered on surveying the grounds for intruders, and a thrice weekly feast. The streets of New Orleans were chock full of interesting game, and true to his word, Dumaine had no trouble supplying his hungry guest and protégé, who by now had become quite proficient in various stalking and killing techniques of his own.

The spring and summer of 1862 witnessed a first at Etenel Babako, the total absence of sugar cane production; this fact that was not lost on Dumaine, and he angrily refused to leave the mansion house except when foraging for food. Although he had long since died, strong emotion stirred within him when it came to anything at his beloved plantation--his own particular passion.

The self imposed confinement did, however, allow him to focus on another serious problem quickly looming on the horizon, John's scheduled return to the Agricultural College upon completion of the fall harvest. The mutually agreed upon 12 month extension would be up then, and there would be no sweet talking or wrangling a second year, to be sure.

The two night feeders fully realized the significance of the impending dilemma, and met on a number of occasions to find a solution to their predicament. They arrived at the same conclusion— John Larson had to die one more time. The question then became: how to do it without arousing suspicion, which would result in the invariable influx of inquisitors, or even worse, family members?

The answer was not far away. The bountiful city of New Orleans had provided a veritable treasure trove of delectable specimens for John's culinary pleasures in the past. Now, it would serve up one of its own to take his place in death.

There was precious little time to waste. Dumaine took wing night after night along the River Road, and always headed straight for Jackson Square, or the venerable Plaza d' Armas, as he preferred to call it, near the banks of the Mississippi. There was no doubt in his mind that he could uncover a suitable replacement. The evening streets teemed with drunken, carousing mortals like salmon working their way upstream, despite the magnificent presence of the St. Louis Cathedral, which quietly beckoned to the lost souls.

Dumaine always stared at the cathedral with revulsion and hate, spitting lustily in the direction of the church spires. It was the only time that he felt unclean, and he did not relish the sensation. Nevertheless, this was the center of his prime hunting grounds, and he needed to take full advantage of it before their window of opportunity had run out.

One night, he began his walk along Decatur Street from the old canal to Esplanade Avenue, then worked his way slowly back on Chartres Street. There were plenty of sweet meats along the way, but as was usually the case, none quite matched John's physical description.

Dumaine did stop for a meal near the Casa Curial; he had hoped that it would have been one of the Capuchin monks who had originally inhabited the structure, but they had vacated in favor of the present courthouse, so he was forced to settle on a fat constable instead. He squealed like a piglet from start to finish, and the old night creature basked in the poor man's fear and desperation.

After several hours of fruitless hunting, Dumaine was about to give up when he finally spotted his mark on the corners of Bourbon and St. Peter's Streets. He fit John's description in every detail—about 20 years old, six feet tall, slim, back hair, with blue eyes and a fair complexion. As an added bonus, the man had just exited a tavern and was staggering toward Dauphine Street, away from the more populous area of the square.

That would make the actual snatch and flight a bit easier, but just as Dumaine quickened his pace and was about to close in on the unsuspecting mortal, he suddenly heard a familiar female voice, one that made even him cringe, if ever so slightly.

"Why, Jacques Dumaine, what a thoroughly pleasant surprise. It is so good to see you again. How HAAAAVE you been?" He glanced mournfully across the street to see a well dressed couple walking arm in arm towards him. The woman seemed to be urging her companion along like an impatient owner tugging at a sniffing dog.

Dumaine was momentarily incensed; after months of long and fruitless searching, his intended prey was getting away! He was in no mood for a prolonged chat, especially with the likes of Lucinda Noonan. But before he could issue the perfunctory return salutations, she blubbered on.

"I was telling James here just the other day that it was high time we paid a visit to your plantation and that student from Pennsylvania that you have staying with you. John Larson is his name, is it not?"

Dumaine regained control of his anger and decided to make an honest effort to be civil; he attempted to reply cordially in the affirmative, but he was only able to move his lips for a mere split second before Lucinda continued with rapid fire precision.

"Why yes, of course it is. How could someone forget such a nice, haaaandsome young man? Did I mention that my cousin Tallulah from Natchitoches will be arriving for a visit next week? It would be a wonderful opportunity to get those two together socially, if you catch my drift. How do you feel about it, Jacques? Care to engage in a bit of matchmaking?

He stared at the woman disbelievingly for a moment; Dumaine fully expected her to turn beet red and pass out on the sidewalk. He was genuinely unaware that anyone could say so much, and so quickly, without taking a breath. The awkward silence was soon broken by the forgotten husband, who eyed Dumaine with no small amount of suspicion.

"Hello, Jacques. How goes things at Etenel Babako?"

"Just fine, James. Glad to see that you are looking well. I trust that the banks of Baton Rouge have been thriving under your stewardship?"

"Work was much less complicated before all this secession nonsense, Jacques. I wish that it had never happened. Banks in the South are not as solvent as their Northern counterparts. We must tread lightly, lest our entire economy collapses before this conflict is resolved."

Dumaine smiled. "I was always under the impression that war was good for business, James."

"Good for some people, yes, the profiteers, the gougers, those trading illegally with the enemy. Before the war we had a perfect arrangement, Jacques. The South possessed the agricultural commodities, while the North could be relied upon for all types of manufactured goods and raw materials."

Noonan shook his head. "United, we were a force to be reckoned with internationally. The rest of the world may not have liked us, but they respected and feared us. Now, the future is uncertain, and all because of this damned fixation on our peculiar institution. It is truly a shame, perhaps....even a sin."

Lucinda piped in. "Politics and business, that's all you men talk about; what of our social visit, gentlemen? Shall we agree on a day?"

For once in his life, James Noonan was actually happy with his wife's interjection. Dumaine had inadvertently diverted him from his intended subject. He too desired to see John, but not as a future member of the family. He wanted to make sure that the boy was safe and sound.

There was still something about Jacques Dumaine that frightened him, but he could not put his finger on it.

"That might not be a bad idea after all, Jacques. It is nearly time to go over your accounts and holdings. Perhaps a trip to your home should be arranged in the near future. We could mix business with pleasure."

Dumaine shook his head sadly. "Unfortunately, madam, I thought it best to send the young man home immediately after the firing on the fort in Charleston Harbor. Your matchmaking will have to be postponed indefinitely."

"Oh, dear," Lucinda moaned. "Tallulah was so looking forward to meeting John. I took the liberty of telling her all about him; I believe she was quite interested."

"So…he is gone then" James echoed thankfully.

"Oh, yes, he most certainly is," Dumaine answered straight faced. "You must excuse me, now. I would like to chat longer but I have a pressing engagement. James, I believe that I will be in Baton Rouge within the next several weeks. I will contact you when I have firmed up the date. We can get together over drinks some evening and discuss my finances then, agreed?"

"Agreed; come along Lucinda. Let's not keep Mr. Dumaine any longer. Good evening to you, sir."

Dumaine bowed slightly. "Good evening, James…Lucinda."

Now it was Mr. Noonan who pulled his reluctant wife along. Dumaine sensed his moment of opportunity and walked ahead as quickly as he dared. All was not lost after all. As he made his way up Dauphine Street, he focused on the grating sounds of a drunken man singing The Maid of Amsterdam at the top of his lungs to no one in particular.

It was the intended victim, inadvertently giving away his location. The fates were indeed kind to Dumaine, if not to John's body double. When they had both nearly reached Burgundy Street, Dumaine seized his chance and jumped the man from behind, sending both crashing downward into the street.

The drunkard's head hit the ground hard, rendering him unconscious, another stroke of luck for Dumaine. Now he did not have to truss him up completely, but merely bind the man's hands behind his back. That was quickly accomplished, and with a glance up and down the street, Dumaine took to the air, heading back to Etenel Babako.

On the long journey back, the unfortunate man regained his senses, but limited as they were due to large quantities of rum, he proved little more than an annoyance to his captor, who carried him like a newborn. The Maid of Amsterdam continued to be sung so wretchedly that the old night creature almost wished for a psalm.

John and Algernon were waiting anxiously in the guest house when Dumaine finally arrived near dawn with his prey, who was now quite sober and screaming for Jesus Christ to save him.

"I think Jesus has more important things to do at the moment." John said without emotion. "Some other time, perhaps."

Algernon stepped forward and grabbed the man tightly by the throat with both hands. The pleading stopped in mid scream, but the squirming did not. After a long half a minute, the bulging eyed, red faced form ceased all movement and was lowered to the ground. He had been throttled into unconsciousness.

"Be Careful, Algernon," Dumaine said cautiously. "Make sure that you do not kill him yet. There is still much to be done."

The overseer reluctantly loosened his grip on the limp figure beneath him. He had been enjoying himself immensely. John stripped the young man down to his drawers, then gathered some of his own clothing and re-dressed him. Algernon furnished a long length of rope and twirled it around the body from shoulders to feet, leaving about 10 foot section of free slack. John paused a moment for one last look, and smiled approvingly. Yes, he would do quite nicely.

Algernon unceremoniously dumped the would-be victim in a work cart that had been placed in front of the guest house; he then hopped on board and guided the mules toward the Mississippi. The two night creatures calmly watched as their trusted servant disappeared from view to complete his assigned task. The impending rising sun would prevent them from any further assistance; their particular limitations forbade it. They shook hands and parted for a well deserved rest, pleased that their plan was moving towards fruition.

The overseer reached the river, and tugged at the reins of the two mules pulling the cart; it came to an abrupt halt. He hopped over the buckboard, stepped to the rear and kicked the now conscious young man along until he fell out of the cart and to the ground; then Algernon jumped down and dragged him by the slack of the rope to the riverbank.

It took only an instant of clarity for the young man to realize what was to follow. He squirmed frantically in a futile attempt to break free, but he was securely bound and had no chance whatsoever. Algernon picked him up like a sack of grain and dumped him into the river while keeping a tight hold of the slack on the rope.

The body plunged down beneath the surface of the water, then the swift current immediately took the man a good five feet away. But he quickly bobbed up! This was an unanticipated delight. Algernon thought that the victim would stay submerged until he drowned, but this would provide a much better show. Now he would simply watch until exhaustion did the trick and forced him under.

Unable to use his hands or feet, the young man screamed and thrashed about wildly, trying desperately to stay above the surface. Algernon thought he behaved like a frightened fish. The screams soon turned to coughs as the waves lapped over his head repeatedly. The last thing the young man saw in this life was the laughing face of the overseer as he dipped under for the last time.

The show was over much too quickly to suit Algernon's taste; he sighed and reeled the body in and back to the shore. "That was a noble effort, sir; you are to be congratulated, but I wish you could have gone on for just a bit longer. Your work is over, but now mine begins."

He put the body into a small rowboat that had been moored nearby, then worked the boat underneath the dock and dropped anchor. He sat the corpse up and lashed it loosely to a piling in mid span. When it was reasonably secure, Algernon slowly got out of the boat and into the water with body alongside. He then lowered the remains well below the water line.

When he was satisfied with the proper depth, he tightened the rope and lashed the body securely to the piling. A week of natural decomposition would now begin, while also allowing the river's rapacious indigenous population to feed on a luscious new food source. The result would make a positive identification virtually impossible, even to Mr. and Mrs. Larson.

Timing was becoming critical, however. Algernon brought the boat to shore, and took a pick from the back of the cart. He gouged several large holes in the side of the boat, finally setting the tiny craft adrift in the river, where it was quickly caught by the current and sank beneath the water. Now that dawn had arrived, the theatrics would take center stage.

He went directly to the stables, saddled a horse, and headed straight for the local authorities in Baton Rouge. The tale he recited at police headquarters, surrounded by curious onlookers while wearing his still damp clothes, was certainly a plausible one. He and John were enjoying some pre-dawn fishing on the river when a submerged tree limb that had gotten caught within the always dangerous Mississippi current struck their small boat, gouged a hole in its side, and caused it to capsize.

The story would not have a happy ending. Algernon sorrowfully relayed how he fought desperately to stay afloat and somehow made it to shore, exhausted. John, on the other hand, was seen to be swept down river and presumed drowned. Of course, for proper effect, it was mentioned that Mr. Dumaine had quickly roused the overseers for a rescue effort, but boats launched to scour the sandbars and shoreline were fruitless.

James Hogan was the police chief of Baton Rouge. He was an ambitious man who advanced more through political patronage than actual hard work; he was also quite taken with his limited capabilities, so it came to no surprise that he swallowed the story, as Algernon would later relate mischievously-- hook, line, and sinker. In the chief's defense, there was no real reason not to. Under Hogan's direction, a poorly organized search was initiated, which was exactly what Dumaine had expected from him.

After five days of fruitless hunting on the part of the local constabulary and some well meaning volunteers, Algernon secretly hauled up the bloated corpse during the night and ferried it a few miles down river, where he snagged it on an uprooted tree that had found a new home on a sand bar.   The body was finally sighted the next day by a passing paddle wheeler.

Letters of condolences were immediately dispatched by Dumaine to John's family and the administrators at the college, informing them of the unfortunate drowning accident, and advising the stunned Larsons' that their son's body was being transported back to York for proper burial, courtesy of the grieving plantation owner, who wrote that he felt somehow responsible for the young man's death. Dumaine mentioned it was the least he could do under the circumstances.

The murder plot concluded without a hitch. The unsuspecting coroner had no doubt that the incident was nothing more than another fatal boating accident on the Mississippi; the remains were sent back by train to Pennsylvania with a respectful suggestion that the casket not be opened due to the poor condition of the body, and for fear of upsetting friends and family further.

That suggestion was initially rejected, but the corpse's ravaged condition nevertheless squelched any misgivings about a false identification from the parents. The unfortunate John Larson was laid to an untimely rest in York Cemetery with all due religious trappings of finality and mourning. Although Dumaine remained on the plantation, he was certain that the ceremonies were better than anything the anonymous filthy drunkard would ever have received in New Orleans, so he actually should have been thankful.

Thoroughly assured that all aspects of the plan were successfully completed, John turned his full attention to a fall and winter conversion of the rice fields. Rice water weevils had thoroughly infested the paddies over a number of years, damaging the rice hulls, and necessitating a changeover to soybeans. This meant draining hundreds of acres of its water, a task that Algernon undertook with relish. He took the utmost pleasure in watching the poor slaves wallow in the muddy fields day after day as they struggled to remove the irrigation ditches and lower the water levels.

But John was no longer interested in their welfare; his only concern over the next five months was that the soil preparations would be finished prior to the spring planting, and he did not care how that was accomplished. The darkies were worked mercilessly, but that was their lot, and John had grown accustomed to their misery. The preparations were completed. Soybeans replaced the Louisiana rice in April of 1863, with only the smaller cornfield acreage remaining extant, much to Dumaine's delight.

The crop rotation was going along splendidly, and he could not have been more pleased with the initial results. Once the sweet potato and soybean crops became firmly established, they would aid in the replenishment of the soil's lost nutrients after a number of harvests. When in the years to come subsequent tests performed by John demonstrated that those same fields had recovered enough to return them to sugar cane production, Dumaine was prepared to be true to his word, and release John from his servitude.

Jacques Dumaine had due cause to be pleased with himself for a variety of reasons. First, his initial gamble of choosing John as the field student had proven correct; second, the decision to kill, transform, and thereby force him into an extended stay was, in his own mind, a stroke of genius; third, the successful faked death scheme effectively ended all threat from outside interference; and finally, the crop rotation changeover was proceeding ahead of even his optimistic timetable.

Perhaps within a 10 year span, the healthy return of his beloved sugar cane could begin once again. With the plantation largely self sufficient, and situated in a location that lent itself to near isolation, there were no indications that anyone or anything from the outside could bring down Dumaine's plan.

However, it was a cruel twist of fate that brought the unfortunate John Larson to Etenel Babako, and eventually morphed him into a grotesque and soulless being. Fate would soon attempt to balance the scales in some small degree with an encounter that would propel him towards his true destiny, a destiny that would help shape the future of the United States.

Chapter 11

The Passion Revealed

John hovered over the now thoroughly familiar landscape of fields, trees, and outbuildings that made up the essence of Etenel Babako. After an extended stay of over two years, he knew exactly where he was despite the heavy winds, intermittent rain, and midnight's black shroud.

The weather was too inhospitable; there would be no unfortunate, River Road stragglers stumbling around the grounds this night to toy with, he thought to himself ruefully. As he made a final pass towards the river, he spied the lights of a sternwheeler that had just come around a bend and was approaching the shore. Perhaps something along the lines of a late night supper would be a distinct possibility after all.

The white, four tiered steamboat belched black smoke from the port and starboard stacks. In the pilot house on the top deck, its skipper worked the vessel smartly alongside the plantation's dock despite the weather's obvious hardships.

While the ship was being properly tethered by several seedy looking hands, additional members of the crew quickly hopped off the side of the main deck. They held unlit hurricane lamps in their hands, which were soon fired up as they worked their way up and down the dock. The men began to use the light from the lamps to inspect the boat's wooden hull all along its water line.

The gangplank was dropped unceremoniously with a crash. Anxious passengers began to exit quickly like steers from a corral as they headed for shore, all the while keenly observing the expressions on the faces of the crewmen working the dock.

John emerged from the darkness and approached a group of men standing off to the right by the plantation's sugar mill. They seemed to be shunned by the rest of the passengers, who either ignored them completely, or addressed them, when necessary, only in the most formal and inhospitable tones. He saw that they wore what appeared to be the blue military uniforms of the United States.

One fat, extremely well dressed civilian passenger with a top hat and gold watch fob sticking out of his vest held a newspaper rolled up in his right hand; he was slapping it inside the palm of his left, while making his point to a lovely young Southern belle in a yellow hoop skirt, who stood by holding her parasol and listening with rapt attention. John casually sidled up to them and listened in on the conversation.

"I tell you, my dear, the war will be over by Thanksgiving, and all of our brave boys will come home. I can feel it. Now that Lee has taken his army north, the Yankees will know what it is like to be violated." He wagged the newspaper in the air. "Robert Rhett's editorial is right and true. Let our soldier's burn THEIR houses, eat THEIR grain and steal THEIR livestock." He looked to the girl for an approving look, received it, and then continued on.

"The Pennsylvania farmlands are rich and plentiful. Once our army has had its fill, it will be on to Baltimore, or even Washington, by God. I would pay to see that gawky, nigger lovin' Lincoln sneak out of the White House, maybe even disguised in a shawl and Scotch cap, just like he did when he snuck his way in."

The belle laughed in agreement at the very thought of it, then looked cautiously at the solders to her left to make sure that they had not been too loud. John could not believe what he had just heard. He did not know this Lee person that the man spoke of, but it sounded as though hostilities had broken out quite some time ago between the North and the South. Could the unthinkable have happened while he had been bound to Etenel Babako?

He had to learn more! Getting information directly from the passengers was not a viable option. If a civil war was indeed raging at that very moment, any normal person would have knowledge of it by now. Stupid questions would draw attention, and it was always best to remain inconspicuous.

John decided to take a more round about approach. "I have not read that particular editorial, sir," he said politely. "Would you mind if I had a look at your newspaper? The article sounds interesting, to say the least."

"By all means, sir," responded the fat man, ignoring the obvious fact that John did not have a Southern accent. "You may keep it."

"You are most kind, sir," returned John. As soon as he had the newspaper in his hand, he asked a second, more pressing question.

"What do you think the inspection of the ship's hull will find?"

"Nothing, I sincerely hope. I spoke to the first mate before we got off. The boat scraped a sand bar about a mile back; he felt that it would be best to check for damage at a mooring, rather than discover a leak while traveling on this blasted river. She's very unforgiving, the Mississippi. Now that I think of it, these wooden paddleboats are like the Yankee armies, impressive looking, but not very strong."

He looked back to the dock. "Hello, there! Are you workmen done with your inspections? I have a pressing business engagement early tomorrow, and I must get downriver shortly. How have we fared?"

"Nothing serious, your lordship," one of the deckhands replied sarcastically. He gave the pilot a wave, and a long, smoke spitting toot from the ship's whistle beckoned passengers and crew back on board.

"These river sailors are a surly lot," the embarrassed fat man muttered to no one in particular. "Well, we'd best get back on board. After you, my dear."

While the passengers began to bunch together as they headed towards the dock, John stood perfectly still, then seized the moment and turned back into the darkness unobserved. He headed straight to the guest house. He angrily brushed off all of his charts and test tubes from the work table onto the floor, and spread the newspaper out on top. The muscles in his body began to tighten.

It was a copy of the Charleston Mercury dated June 18th, 1863. John began scanning the stories crammed amid the tiny, printed columns. To his shock, there was an article stating that portions of The Army of Northern Virginia had emerged from the Blue Ridge Mountains, and had crossed the Potomac River on June 15th, heading through Maryland and towards the Cumberland Valley.

Another story continued to praise the bold leadership of Generals Robert E. Lee and Stonewall Jackson following their rout of the bumbling Fighting Joe Hooker and his Army of the Potomac the month before at Chancellorsville. John had never heard of that locale, so he could not even figure out what state it was in, although he surmised that the battle may have been in Virginia.

A final scan pinpointed an article by the editor of the newspaper, Robert Rhett, referencing the impending "European" recognition, following a sure victory on Northern soil, and the subsequent intervention into the war on behalf of the Confederate States of America.

John was certain that European recognition could only point towards England and France. Both nations would reap great benefits from a weakened and fragmented rival the likes of the United States. They must be waiting patiently like circling buzzards for one last Southern victory to formally announce their intentions.

He pounded the table sharply with both fists. It was as he initially feared when he was back at the Agricultural College. A war had broken out; the Republic was in danger of total collapse! He seethed with rage at the thought that pig-headed Southern fire eaters and self righteous New England abolitionists had triggered such an abominable situation. His mind raced wildly. Maryland had been invaded, with his native Pennsylvania soon to follow.

From what he was able to gather from the general tone of the paper, the war had been going badly for the North, at least in the east, for quite some time. John once again visualized the United States in mortal danger of an irrevocable split; he knew that he must do SOMETHING!

He was so totally wrapped up in his thoughts that he initially did not notice the intense waves of patriotic fervor swelling in his cold, dead breast. It had been a long time since he had felt anything other than instincts relating to survival and the thrill of the kill.

Then, as in an epiphany, it suddenly occurred to John that he had finally found his one, true passion. He did not know what it was at the time of his transformation because Louisiana had only announced its secession from the United States two months before his arrival to Etenel Babako; at that time, everyone was wading in murky, uncharted waters.

He bolted out the front door and raced for the main house. Dumaine was languishing in his favorite rocking chair on the second floor balcony when John arrived. This time, however, it was John who jumped, up onto the second floor veranda.

"The deception is over, Dumaine. I have discovered my passion. I go now to fight for my country before all is lost. The terms of my servitude are hereby broken. I leave tonight."

Dumaine was totally dumbfounded by this sudden turn of events, but he knew that there was absolutely nothing that he could do to stop John from abandoning the plantation. He rose from his rocking chair, took a few steps closer, and looked into the eyes of his fellow night creature.

"So, you have found out at last," he spoke dejectedly as he let out a long sigh. "For two long years I have kept the war hidden from you. That was no easy task, considering that on the night of our first meeting hostilities began in earnest. Do you remember the mysterious rider that interrupted our dinner? He was spreading the word of our attack on the Federal stronghold in Charleston Harbor, your Fort Sumter."

John thought back. "Yes, yes. I do remember it. Was that truly the start of the war?"

"Indeed," Dumaine responded sadly. "I had an uneasy premonition that the war might point you to your passion. Unfortunately, it would appear that I was correct. It was the general consensus that this conflict could not last for more than a few months, but we all have underestimated the resolve on both sides."

"In fact," Dumaine announced with some degree of trepidation, "the state of Louisiana has been in Northern hands for some time now."

"How can that be?" John asked wide eyed. "Your plantation has not suffered in the least. The slaves remain as your chattel, and the property has not been molested in any shape or form."

Dumaine laughed heartily. "I took their ridiculous Oath of Allegiance while last in Baton Rouge to save my lands. What do I care for the North, or the South for that matter, when Etenel Babako is all that I truly desire in the world? Your President Lincoln's proclamation emancipating the slaves left me no other alternative. The plantation cannot be properly run without their strong backs and weak minds. With this oath, I have bought myself precious time."

John was puzzled. "What do you mean?"

Dumaine smiled. "All Southerners in those areas of rebellion who reject the notion of an independent Confederacy may retain their lands and slaves. It is all so very convenient."

"That is all the more reason that you should welcome my departure, Dumaine. If the South were to prevail, I fear things would go hard on you. Perhaps my participation can perform some good service to the North."

"Do not overestimate your powers, my impetuous Yankee. You may be killed any number of ways, as you well know." Dumaine was now speaking not as an opponent, or even a master, but as a true friend. John instinctively understood this and listened attentively.

"If you proceed on this path, you will encounter those who know of our existence, and especially our weaknesses. We are so reviled, feared, and misunderstood that there are those on BOTH sides who would gladly band together to dispatch you from this world with great satisfaction, regardless of your sympathies." John lowered his head, knowing that the words spoken by Dumaine were entirely correct.

"My advice to you is to trust no living man, woman, or child…and there is one last thing." Dumaine's facial expression slowly changed from one of brotherly concern to that of fear. This was the one and only time that John had observed fright in his mentor, and he was startled by it.

"Your particular passion will most certainly overlap the boundaries of our Code. Night creatures may select the dregs of human society for subsistence purposes. The only other exceptions would be to repel an impending attack, or to insure a creature's anonymity and survival. Direct interference into the affairs of mankind, particularly an intrusion that results in death and destruction, is strictly forbidden."

John became mildly annoyed. "This is nothing new, Dumaine. You explained all this to me in the library after I transformed. What is your point? If I do in fact break our code, it will be for the best of intentions, and not out of malice."

Dumaine replied ominously. "Good intentions will avail you nothing. What I did not tell you previously is that there are a select handful of night creatures that call themselves the Council of Djadadjii. They are very old, and very wise. Once it is determined that a transgression has been committed, the offending creature…disappears, and is never heard from again. That is the fate you may well encounter. Now that you know the FULL story, go and find your destiny."

He paused for a moment, and then finished with a threat. "And rest assured, if the armies of either country are unfortunate enough to penetrate the boundaries of Etenel Babako, they will pay dearly for defiling MY passion."

John smiled briefly, then leaped over the railing to the ground below. The fat businessman's newspaper was dated June 15th; that was four full days ago. He would take to the winds to reach this Army of Northern Virginia, but even so, the journey might take much longer than expected.

He would also need to find adequate shelter each night before dawn until he reached the familiar surroundings of his native state. That would be no easy task, and it equated to covering hundreds of miles. If he chose his resting place poorly, the sun would burn him to flaming cinders. The safe haven of Etenel Babako could no longer protect him.

There would also be the problem of finding the proper food sources along the way. He would need to feed more often if he was going to reach those rebellious troops in a timely fashion, before they inflicted any more damage. However, he still had to do so with discretion, else suspicion might be aroused.

He looked back up at Dumaine and gave him a parting shout. "I will take my chances. When I feel that my country is safe, I will return to finish the work that I started here. You have my word on it, friend."

Dumaine nodded gratefully; he was deeply touched that Etenel Babako might still have an opportunity to return to its former glory. "Thank you, John, and be careful among the mortals. They are decidedly weaker, but they have strength in numbers." He wanted to say more, but his young apprentice was gone in a flash.

John feverishly worked his way north on his nightly glides, riding on strong wind currents, while finding safe havens in barns, attics, and root cellars during the dangerous daylight hours. He carefully roamed cities the likes of Granada, Memphis, Cairo, Louisville, Cincinnati, and Canton, gathering valuable information about the war, and finding suitable kills as well that would not be missed. John was sure that Dumaine would have been pleased with his selections.

Only when he veered to the east, passed through Pittsburgh, and was deep within his home state, did he feel as though he were nearing the end of his journey, and approaching the start of his own particular contribution to the North's war effort.

John had decided upon a final course of action soon after he left Louisiana. Killing individual soldiers would accomplish very little in the grand scheme of things. First of all, from what information he had picked up on the way, this General Robert E. Lee had over 75,000 troops in his Army of Northern Virginia. There were only so many men even a night creature could kill from dusk to dawn.

Also, multiple kills on a recurring basis behind their own lines would send a danger signal to the despised Freemasons, who doubtless were scattered throughout the ranks of these Rebels. John had to avoid them whenever possible. Only the Masons had hard evidence of his kinds' existence, so they truly believed that such creatures existed; coupled with that evidence and belief was the knowledge and wisdom necessary to destroy him.

He decided on a safer and possibly more devastating plan--to target the upper echelon of the Rebel army. If he could eventually locate high ranking officers, and then partially disable them by secretly drawing enough of their blood, the subsequent weakness in mind and body could adversely affect their ability to properly lead and direct troops during an engagement.

Their clouded judgment could ultimately result in the death of thousands of fellow Rebels at the hands of Northern forces, perhaps even deciding the final outcome of a major battle. Furthermore, his presence would remain unknown, allowing him to continue his hunting until the Federal Army of the Potomac could gather enough confidence to stand on its own without his help.

When John eventually picked up the trail of the Confederate horde in the Cumberland Valley, it had split into several sections, initially causing him much distress as to which column to target first. Fortunately, the Army of Northern Virginia shortly thereafter began a consolidation of forces in the general area of Cashtown and Gettysburg. It was now the end of June.

John was quite pleased with this development. He had lived just a few short miles away to the east in nearby York, and he had spent several summers working in Gettysburg, so he knew the town and the surrounding area quite well. This would prove advantageous for quick kills and safe harbors at night. After weighing the pros and cons, John decided that he would make his first contact at Cashtown.

Chapter 12

The Plan Unfolds

John's thoughts snapped back to the present as he stepped from the porch through the front door of the Cashtown Hotel, one of several headquarters for Confederate forces in the area around Gettysburg. He knew that he must be extremely careful. The orderly who had just admitted him under the false pretext of delivering an important message to the commanding officer wore a hated Masonic symbol on his vest.

The members of that secret society gave off the scent of rotting meat to night creatures; it was a form of built in alarm system to detect those men who did not display their insignias prominently. John willed himself to avoid gagging in the orderly's presence, lest he give away his disguise. Unless he did something obvious, he could quite possibly remain undetected by this scum.

"I'll take the message," the man said curtly as he held out his hand with anticipation. "I give you my personal guarantee that General Hill will receive it."

John now knew whom he was targeting; he had a split second decision to make. His choice was to either kill anyone who got in his way at the hotel until he located this General Hill and incapacitated him, or to continue his bold bluff to its fruition. Unfortunately, he was at a distinct disadvantage. He was blind as to the interior layout of the hotel, and he had no inkling just how many soldiers were quartered inside for that matter.

Pistols would have no lasting effect on him, other than the temporary pain and jolt to his system, but the loud crack of gunfire, along with the resulting shouts of alarm, would most certainly rouse many in the surrounding encampments. All of his work up to this point would be ruined, and his identity would most certainly be exposed. No, John had come this far on a ruse; to continue it was the only viable option left open.

"There is no written message," he replied formally. "It is a verbal directive from General Lee himself, and I was instructed to give it to General Hill personally."

The orderly began to look at him with suspicion, unconvinced of the validity of his statement. Since there was no contact with the enemy at the moment, the employment of verbal directives seemed out of place. John continued to spin his tale.

"We are in hostile territory; the fear was that written correspondence could provide damaging information if it were to fall into the wrong hands." He paused to let his explanation sink in. "Now that you are aware of the situation, I need to speak with General Hill AT ONCE, do you understand?"

Now the shoe was on the other foot. It was the orderly who was under pressure, and the man was definitely not up to meeting the challenge. John was sure that his own convincing theatrics were worthy of the great John Wilkes Booth himself.

Of course, the magical name of Lee helped fluster the orderly into a panic and ultimate submission. "Yes…by all means," he said meekly. "The general is this way; if you would follow me, please." He spun around, hurried through the hallway, and started up the staircase, with John following at a respectable distance continuing with his official airs.

Once he had an opportunity to briefly scan the first floor, John realized it was a good thing that the orderly had buckled under after all. A sitting and dining room on either side of the front hallway revealed a slew of dusty, tired officers sleeping soundly on winged back chairs, couches, and even tables. There was no telling how many soldiers were upstairs as well. Killing all of them quickly and quietly would have been a highly unlikely scenario.

There were four bedrooms on the second floor. Two were situated directly towards the rear of the house, while the remaining bedrooms had window views looking out onto the main road. The orderly ventured towards the front of the hotel and the bedroom on the far left; he stopped and then knocked lightly on the door. When there was no immediate reply, he knocked a bit louder.

"Yes, what is it?" an irritable, sleepy voice was heard from within.

The orderly leaned close to the door and responded contritely. "Beggin' yur pardn, genral, but there's a courier here with an urgent message from Genral Lee. He says that he was ordered to give it to you himself."

"Send him in then" replied the hidden voice, "and check to see if there's any of that fine coffee left; haven't had coffee this good in months."

The orderly opened the door, stepped to the side as John entered the bedroom, and then closed it afterwards. John could hear the sound of the man's footsteps trail off as he made his way downstairs to search for the precious dark brew.

In the center of the small room stood a square table covered by numerous maps, with several rickety chairs positioned nearby, a pair of field glasses slung over the back of one, and a fine looking gray uniform blouse with gold stars on the lapels draped over the other.

A well worn dresser and bureau were positioned up against the wall on the right; a four poster pine bed was on the left, with its dingy white sheets kicked off the edge and sprawling onto the floor. The windows were open to let in any possible breeze, although the drooping light brown curtains announced that none was to be had at the moment.

A thin, frail looking man of about 40 years of age sat up on the edge of the bed in his stocking feet. After a moment's hesitation, he stood up and arched his back; the joints made slight cracking sounds as the man winced. John was sure this was the same officer that he had seen earlier in the evening giving orders on the front porch. He recognized the distinctive red calico shirt that seemed to drape over him.

It was almost as though this general was inviting the enemy to take notice of him. However, up close and in the light, the man was certainly not an imposing figure, to say the least; he barely filled out his gray uniform pants. John felt a tinge of admiration for this soldier, despite his misguided allegiance. He was undoubtedly a general who directed his troops from the front, not the safety of the rear.

John's second observation was that although undoubtedly handsome at one time, this officer was presently in very poor health. His face was pasty and gaunt, and his eyes, although they retained a slight sparkle, appeared sunken in his skull; the nose was thin and sharp. He had a full beard and a slick-backed, reddish colored mop of hair that was parted on his left side, and extended well over his ears.

The soldier began to inch forward and took hold of one of the bedposts for quick support. His movements were akin to so many of the drunks and derelicts that Dumaine often targeted in New Orleans or Baton Rouge for John's consumption. "All right, man, out with it," he said with some authority. "What is the message from General Lee?"

John felt that he had to come up with something non-controversial for General Hill while his heightened sense of hearing strained to listen for unwanted footsteps in the hall and adjacent rooms. Under the precarious circumstances, he blurted out: "The commanding general sends his compliments, and wishes to remind you that his most recent orders are still in place, and that you are to proceed as planned."

John was now certain that they would not be interrupted; his eyes turned a deep, scarlet red, fixing a hypnotic gaze upon the puzzled officer. The man froze in his tracks before he could let out another word. John walked over slowly, and with one hand, grasped him by his red shirt and tipped him back onto the bed like a falling tree.

He straddled over his would-be victim, and once in position, deftly exposed the man's already scrawny neck. It was his original intention to drink deeply, but when John got down to the actual business of feeding, he drew back swiftly in disgust, brought his hand to his mouth, and choked.

This man was not merely ill; he was slowly dying. His blood had the taste of spoiled milk. It took great force of will for John to complete the important task that he had come for. Fortunately, this particular Rebel's weakened condition also meant that less blood needed to be withdrawn in order to have the desired effect of temporary mental and physical fatigue.

After a nauseating minute that felt decidedly longer, John rose up and turned away with relief. He took out a raggedy handkerchief from his back pocket and softly dabbed the general's pencil thin neck until the bleeding stopped. Glancing about the room, he got some water from a basin on the bureau and cleansed the wound until only two tiny, pin prick bite marks remained.

There would be no tell-tale signs that anything out of the ordinary had occurred at this headquarters. The man was already sick before his arrival, so any further deterioration in his condition would seem to be a natural regression. John wondered if this general would be of any use at all in the coming battle.

Once he was satisfied with the officer's positioning, John promptly left the room and shut the door quietly behind him, gliding lightly passed the other three bedrooms. No one else had been awakened or alarmed by his visit. He reached the head of the stairs and started down just as the faithful orderly was walking back up with a large pot of steaming coffee. John held his breath once more to keep from gagging at the approaching stench of rotting meat.

The private missed his only opportunity for recognition when he failed to notice that John cast no reflection on the gleaming pot as he passed him on the stairs, although he did stop briefly in mid-stride to turn and watch John as he left the hotel. There was something about this currier that did not sit right with the orderly.

Try as he might, he could not quite identify what it was exactly, but he was sure that it was of some importance. The orderly shrugged his shoulders and continued on his way up the stairs with the coffee for his woozy commander, who was now in desperate need of some fluids.

John lost no time walking off of the main road and back into the safety of the nearby woods. Everything had fallen into place for him this time, but he knew that he had been extremely lucky. The two sentinels out front had no time to send an alarm before he had crushed their skulls and hidden their bodies in the nearby ditch. Without the obvious signs of a struggle, their absence would be interpreted as an act of desertion or dereliction of duty. In either case, John was safe from detection, for the moment.

It was also a great relief that the general was alone in the room when John arrived. The glaring lack of effect that point blank range pistol fire would have had on him would most certainly have alerted those damned Freemasons, who always seemed to appear at the most inopportune times for his kind.

John did not have to look at his pocket watch to know that this night was drawing to a close. It would be dawn in a few precious hours, not enough time to continue the hunt without taking another great personal risk, and he did not wish to tempt fate. Under the circumstances, he thought it best to find some secure shelter from the sun's searing rays sooner rather than later.

He decided to proceed directly into Gettysburg, a place out of his not too distant past. No serious clashes had taken place there as of yet, although from a bird's eye view, which a night creature had the luxury of having, it was apparent that two opposing armies could very well bump into each other in that quiet, unsuspecting town.

But before striking out for Gettysburg and safety, John realized that his system could take no more. He clutched at his stomach with his right hand, leaned against a huge boulder with his left, and then doubled over, vomiting up the tainted blood of the sickly General Hill. He wondered whether or not he had drawn out too much.

When his convulsions were complete, John straightened up and took a deep breath. Despite his transformation, he had still retained the old habit of trying his best not to throw up even though he knew that he would feel better after he did. He wiped his mouth unceremoniously against his sleeve, and began heading east. "Must have been something I ate," he said to himself.

Chapter 13

Place of Refuge

John morphed into his wolfish shape and kept to the dense greenwood parallel to the main road, traveling in an easterly direction on the Chambersburg Pike until he ventured into sleepy, unsuspecting Gettysburg. Upon reaching its outskirts, he regained human form and made his way towards the town center, which the local inhabitants had colloquially dubbed "the diamond" because of its unique shape. This landmark enabled him to regain his bearings in the dark.

As he trudged along on the sidewalk, looking slowly from side to side, the familiar sights on Baltimore Street, with its wide town dirt roads and crowded brick houses, made him feel much more at ease. It was not long before he stopped to pause at the corner of Baltimore and Middle Streets to gaze briefly at the Fahnestock Dry Goods Store.

This was the place where he had labored for three summers, and the store served him well on several fronts. As a sales clerk, he saved what little money he could in order to help pay for his impending bills at the Agricultural College, and it also enabled him to escape the suffocating atmosphere that his father had created back home.

As town buildings fared, it was not very impressive, just a three storied brick structure with a large "Fahnestock Brothers" sign of black and white painted in big capital letters on the side facing the street. The front of the store had more of a soft, house like appearance, with two small display windows on either side of the small main entrance door.

127

Shuttered windows on the rest of the first and second floors were capped by a sloping roof that took away a portion of the top floor. The remaining portion of the roof was a flat surface, and it provided both a fair view and a fine summer breeze when John and his coworkers would venture up in the early afternoons to share their lunches and elaborate on their plans for the future.

His mind continued to slip back to those times, and to the kindly Mr. Edward Fahnestock and his lovely wife Marie; John had harbored a secret wish of having them as his parents. He always enjoyed their company immensely; the Fahnestock's were a carefree, loving couple, so much the opposite of his own family in York.

There was also the pretty Ginny Wade, a young Gettysburg seamstress who stopped in the dry goods store now and again. John recalled being thoroughly smitten with her at first sight, yet all of his concerted efforts to win her attention and subsequent affection proved futile. But now, there were no longer any feelings good, bad, or otherwise associated with those mortals. All that remained was the knowledge and remembrance of them, and he was not upset with the loss.

He continued on along Baltimore Street, and eventually came upon the houses of David McCreary and Agnes Barr, two regular customers who had taken a liking to the personable young John when he filled their orders at the dry goods store. But neither residence was his personal preference for vital daylight shelter. They would be fall back locations if circumstances went terribly awry.

When he finally passed Breckenridge Street, John knew that his chosen destination was close at hand. A short walk brought him to the house of his cousin, cabinet maker Henry Garlach. Henry had a small shop set up in the back section of the house, while the rest of it acted as the permanent residence for his wife Catherine, along with the children, William and Anna. William had been especially fond of John, and he looked up to him as one would an older brother.

For several years running, John had refused to work with Henry as a carpenter's apprentice. He had the distinct feeling that it would be a way for his parents to spy on him via his well meaning relatives. In his own mind, if he was going to take advantage of being away from home, then he would attempt to stay out of sight as much as possible.

John was able to avoid any bad feelings with the Garlachs' by explaining that a business setting like Fahnestock's would serve him far better in the long run than that of an apprentice position in a skill that he would never make proper use of. However, he gratefully accepted their gracious invitation of free room and board in return for minor chores around the house and back yard.

While he had it in the back of his mind for some time to use the Garlach house as a safe refuge, actual use of the home's interior would be totally out of the question. The diabolical plan set in motion back at Etenel Babako guaranteed that promising young student John Larson would be dead and buried, at least in the hearts and minds of all those who knew him.

No, he had something else in mind. He recalled that there was a two foot high crawl space under the first floor that ran the entire length and width of the home. When the Garlach children played hide and seek with their friends, John would often watch them with amusement; that crawl space was Anna and William's secret hideaway, and they loved the fact that John never revealed its location.

The front and sides of the house were sealed to the ground with stone and mortar for aesthetic reasons; however, the rear portion, the one that faced an enclosed backyard complete with barn, privy, and woodshed, was merely shuttered up with sections of wooden framing that were easily removable.

John had kept a slouch hat that he had taken from one of the unlucky headquarters guards back at Cashtown. He put it on and pulled it down so low that his forehead was nearly obliterated; this was no time to be spotted by any of his insomniac relations making an unscheduled trip to the outhouse.

He swiftly made his way around to the back of the house through a long, thin alleyway that was piled high with crates and discarded wood from Henry's carpentry shop. The remaining portion of the Garlach property was enclosed by seven foot high clapboard fencing, so he had to hop over to reach the back yard.

If he had tried such a maneuver prior to his stay at Etenel Babako, the resulting noise would have frightened the pigs into a squealing frenzy enough to raise the dead, John thought with a tinge of irony. But his enhanced physical powers enabled him to spring over and float to the ground below with barely an effort.

Satisfied that he had not yet been spotted, he glided over to the house and removed one section of wood framing from the small opening under the back porch. Lying on his stomach, he snaked his way in head first, then turned around and carefully reset the framing. When he was satisfied with its positioning, he moved rhythmically towards the front section of the house. It would be darker and safer in that portion of the crawl space.

While on his way there, he encountered several large, brown rats that had wisely decided to take up residence. When he petted them affectionately, they responded in kind, following and snuggling up close to him when he flipped over onto his back for a well deserved rest.

John could finally relax. He happily took in the smell of the rats, the wood foundation, and the soft, cool earth beneath him. He could hear the footsteps of Henry as he clomped across the floor above him, while the rapid pitter patter could only mean little Anna following close behind him. His thoughts then turned to the thousands of rampaging Rebel soldiers bent on wanton destruction in his native state. That image kept him awake longer than he anticipated.

This particular Confederate army had caused a great deal of trouble to the Federals from the start of the insurrection; that was for sure. From what John had been able to learn on his way from Louisiana, courtesy of both Yankee and Rebel newspaper accounts, this General Robert E. Lee and his Army of Northern Virginia had outfought and thoroughly outmaneuvered the well intentioned but bumbling Army of the Potomac.

John could not understand how the military situation had gotten so far out of hand for the United States. He was no soldier, but while at the Agricultural College, he and his classmates had often discussed the overall strengths of the North over the Southern section of the country. Common sense dictated that all the talk of secession and breaking away to form a new country was only that—talk.

There was the obvious overwhelming Northern numerical superiority, followed by a preponderance of mills, foundries, and factories, all filled with scores of skilled workers that would be quite capable of supplying armies in the field. When one included an excellent railroad transportation system able to get men and materials when and where they were needed, it would seem that even if there were a Rebel uprising, it should have been crushed quickly and easily.

All that Dixie seemed to possess in any great abundance was slaves, cotton, and loudmouth extremists who did not represent the feelings of the entire South. But wars are not fought on paper; nor are they won with logic. The more he thought about the situation, the more John came to the inexorable conclusion that the South's greatest asset had to lie in its leadership.

For reasons that he could not understand, Rebel officers, at least in the east, were completely outgeneraling their Yankee counterparts to a complete frazzle. The important question was: why was this happening? Surely both sides boasted of officers that had been schooled via the Military Academy at West Point. They had the same courses, the same instructors, and the same training.

And yet the end results in this war favored the Confederates, at least as far as John knew. He only hoped that Federal forces in other war torn parts of the country were faring better. But hope was not something he could count on. The stakes were much too high; all the more reason for him to believe that his chosen plan of action was the proper one, despite the potential dangers from both the Freemasons, and the elusive Council of Djadadjii.

John would continue in his quest to target and disable as many high ranking Rebel officers as he could find. However, the most important thing at the moment was getting some rest. He extended his hand upwards and briefly touched the wooden floorboards that were no more than a foot from the tip of his nose. He was pleased. It was really all quite cozy when one factored in the excited, red eyed rats scampering over and about him in the darkness, vying for his attention.

This location would remain his first option for daylight sanctuary, that is, if the insurrectionists would show a little cooperation with their movements. Unfortunately, John was unaware of the Rebels true intentions and destinations, much the same as the worried political and military leaders in Washington, D.C.

If in fact there was a sudden movement of gray troops, John would have to abandon the Garlach house and pursue them, but at least they would be easy to track. He really had no choice in the matter, although he did have alternative safe havens in mind as backups outside the town proper.

But when the devil would this oft ridiculed Federal Army of the Potomac strike a blow? And where was it? Could it not even locate and defeat Rebels in one of the Union's most loyal states? If the answer turned out to be no, then the prospects of keeping the Republic together seemed frightfully dismal.

John brought those disturbing questions swirling around in his head to a close. He laced his hands together and placed them over his chest; lying motionless, he slowly closed his eyes. Soon, he was fast asleep, just as the dawn breeze worked its way through the town. Little did he know that his questions would be answered with a vengeance within the next several days.

Chapter 14

An Unlikely Rendezvous

John awoke abruptly to the sounds of loud banging. Startled and disoriented in the dark, he instinctively took a defensive posture; he threw his hands out wide in front of his chest and jerked his body up to regain a sitting position for an impending attack. Could the Freemasons somehow have discovered his existence and whereabouts? How had they tracked him down?

Unfortunately, John had totally forgotten about his sleeping arrangements and close confinement; he instantly banged his head against the underside of the house floorboards. The force of the impact caused him to return unceremoniously to his original position, which was flat out on his back in the dirt.

Lying perfectly still for several seconds, John cleared his head and began to concentrate. The banging sounds continued with a vengeance, and it was then that he remembered his surroundings. Henry Garlach was evidently attempting to finish up some type of cabinetry in his carpentry shop before dinner, for sure.

If John had been able to retain his sense of humor, he might have had a good laugh at his own expense. Dumaine would doubtless have been happy to witness the bumbling show of ineptitude. As it was, he smiled ever so briefly and rubbed the center of his forehead, which would sport a large red knot and then disappear shortly. His elder cousin's strong work ethic had not diminished over the years.

"Thank you very much, Henry," he muttered under his breath with some marked irritation. "Perhaps I should peer through your shop window, tap on the glass, and wave hello. Would your heart stand the shock?" John knew that he could never follow through on the idea, but it was still a delicious fantasy.

He looked around for his new found pets, but the noise had frightened the rats into their underground burrows. He flipped over onto his stomach in the crawlspace and once again made his way towards the rear of the house. Slowly moving the wood framing a few inches forward and to the left, he peeked out at the dusk, spying Henry's wife Catherine exiting the barn with some corn and walking towards the back porch. John saw that she remained a plain, heavily built woman whose major attributes were a kind heart and a strong back.

When he heard her enter the house and announce that supper would be ready shortly, John decided to wait a while longer until darkness had tightened its grip. One thing was for certain; the atmosphere of normality in the Garlach residence was not disrupted by the impending influx of enemy troops. Without additional information, John had to assume that the Rebels he had left back at Cashtown the night before were still bivouacked there.

That was a very interesting development. Nearly a full day had gone by, yet the invaders had not continued to drive eastward. Why did they not simply invest Gettysburg in force and take whatever they needed? After all, they were in hostile territory; surely re-supply by way of Virginia would be a logistical headache.

And yet, the red-shirted Confederate General Hill seemingly did nothing. Then again, perhaps he was expecting additional reinforcements.

Whatever the case, John knew that there would be no serious opposition from area militia against large numbers of heavily armed troops.

John remained in the crawlspace for two more hours, waiting patiently for total darkness, and a lessening of activity in the home above him. The rats finally popped out from their burrows; he gave them a few quick head rubs, then emerged from his hideout and slipped behind the barn. He stretched his arms out and took to the air, ignoring the time wasteful pedestrian mode of travel in favor of one with more speed.

He needed to know what was going on in a hurry if he was to single out an important Rebel, enjoy a light snack, AND return to a place of safety by dawn. While surveying the surrounding area, he was pleased to see that a large unit of Union cavalry was encamped just west of town. Perhaps that was why the Confederates did not attempt a further incursion.

With the Rebels temporarily checked to the west, John decided to scout north of Gettysburg. Hovering just above the tree tops, he remembered that he had another decision to make. Should he follow one of the Mummasburg, Carlisle, and Harrisburg Roads, or the York Pike? There was no time to reconnoiter all four of them at once; they fanned out much too far apart.

On a whim, he chose the Harrisburg Road, but he would not go much farther than Rock Creek. That meant a return trip over one of John's least favorite locales while he was alive, the dumpy little three horse town of Heidlersburg.

He recalled spending a week there one afternoon when directed to make a bulk delivery via horse and cart from Fahnestock's. The few buildings of note were drab and poorly constructed, while the streets were littered with all manner of debris. As to the inhabitants, the men were uniformly cantankerous and cheap; their women, although polite, all looked like 40 miles of corduroy road.

Those things mattered not to the John who was about to make a return visit. His interests were decidedly predatory in nature now, and he was not to be disappointed. Gliding north, it was easy to spot campfires scattered throughout Heidlersburg proper and the surrounding countryside; that certainly meant soldiers, but whose side were they on?

John hoped that they were Federals attempting to encircle Gettysburg. After all, the town was known as a major hub for turnpikes and roads in every direction. From a military standpoint, its possession would be highly desirable. If Union troops could control Gettysburg, it would be much more difficult, not to mention more time consuming, for the Rebels to move about. Perhaps that might put a crimp in their strategy, especially if they had counted on speed as a vital element for success.

Rather than work his way in from the outside through the picket lines, as he had done at Cashtown, John flew straight for the center of town. He set down ever so lightly through an open hayloft door of a large horse barn that looked out onto what was humorously referred to as Main Street.

There was a great deal of commotion below, and it was quite evident that these were enemy troops. John watched the comings and goings for about an hour; he was waiting for the slightest lull in activity. By then, the barn's ground floor was now chockfull of Confederates taking full advantage of a luxurious night's sleep; to soldiers on the move, that equated to a roof above their heads.

Fortunately, none of the men had thought about bedding down in the hayloft above them. It would have been a dicey situation had he stayed in persona and been discovered as John Larson, a Yankee, watching enemy troop movements. And if he chose to remain a night creature, his element of surprise would have been lost amid all those soldiers. This forced him to exit the barn the way he came in, through the air. He had to be careful, however; there were still too many soldiers completing their bivouac for him to be flitting around above roaring campfires.

Lighting down behind a number of supply wagons, he stepped out of the shadows and into the firelight; thus began his search for another high ranking Rebel officer. Moving about proved to be an easier task than originally anticipated; while John grudgingly admitted to himself that these men had demonstrated to be excellent fighters, they were most certainly not Beau Brummels by strict military appearances.

The officers generally wore distinguishing gray uniforms, but the vast majority of the rank and file looked like a motley collection of stumblebums. They wore all manner of tattered, homespun shirts, pants, and hats, while a good number of them were barefoot. John was incredulous; was this ragtag looking group a part of the famous Army of Northern Virginia that had inflicted so much damage to the Union cause?

Fortunately, John fit right in; he had not thought about changing his clothes since he had left Louisiana, and the brief respite underneath his cousin's house left him particularly dusty, with a slight scent of dankness and rot added in for good measure. While he looked and even smelled the part of a veteran, he didn't sound much like one. He had a decidedly poor imitation Southern twang to his speech, so any conversations would have to be short, sweet, and to the point.

John walked toward the town's lone inn, figuring that it would make a good headquarters set up for someone of high authority. The assumption was entirely correct. Guards stood ramrod straight at the front entrance, signaling a ranking personage of some sort, while officers whisked in and out of the front door to waiting horses tied up nearby.

John's previous ruse would not work this time around. It was not late enough in the evening; there were way too many soldiers moving about to slip in undetected. Under the circumstances, he felt that perhaps it would be best to wait and let nature take its course, in every sense of the word.

He walked casually to the rear of the building and waited patiently behind a damaged caisson and limber that was set no more than 20 paces from the inn's privy. Two hours later, a time span that featured a veritable parade of soldiers happily making use of the more civilized municipal accommodations, a smallish looking, gray clad figure with a slight limp in his gait walked out the back door and made his way to the outhouse.

John watched the man with some interest. He had a prominently bald, almost egg-shaped head, which drew further attention to his bulging eyes. A long, flat nose was followed by a goatee accentuated beard, and ears that looked as though they were tilted backwards on an angle.

But the most important aspect of this particular soldier was his uniform. Three gold stars were sewn on the collar of his double buttoned dress coat, a designation of a major general. This would be the one, and now would be the time. John's thoughts were quickly interrupted by a shout from an orderly at the back door of the inn.

"General Ewell, a rider's just arrived with dispatches, sir."

The officer barked out an annoying reply; "Put the goddamn communications on my desk. The war can wait five blasted minutes for a man to relieve himself in peace." The orderly immediately ducked back inside the house as though a mini ball was approaching, while summarily slamming the door shut behind him.

All was quiet once more. John allowed the now muttering officer a moment to enter the outhouse and get down to his personal business, then he made his move. Stepping out from behind the caisson, he rushed forward and swung the door open. There he unceremoniously confronted the startled sitting general, who commenced reciting an interesting string of invectives with a high pitched voice.

Although impressed with the rich, colorful profanities, John could not permit the noise to arouse unwanted attention. He quickly jumped inside and shut the door behind him, placing a hand over the general's mouth. The privy was cramped and foul-smelling, with the door butting up against John's back. He looked down and stared the officer straight in the eyes. The voice became silent, and the body stiffened with fear into a complete paralysis.

John leaned over slightly to begin his feed, placing one hand on the man's leg for support, while tilting the balding head to the side with the other. It was at that moment his hand felt a strange sensation. The general's leg was solid, with no give to it whatsoever. John pressed down harder, but to no avail. Taking another approach, he made a fist and rapped on the leg, and it replied in kind with a sound very much like a knock on a door.

This man's left leg was not flesh and blood, but wood. John wondered how and in what battle the soldier had made that sacrifice, but he could not allow the any feelings to get in the way of his duty, even if he had still possessed them. This man was an important Rebel leading a host of secessionists through a vital section of the country.

John's only regret was that he could not have accosted the general in a more dignified setting. "Sorry, my indisposed friend, but I must take advantage of any opportunity that presents itself. I cannot be sure if a better one will ever come along."

He drank deeply, and then slowly cracked open the door of the privy to see if there was anyone anxiously awaiting his turn. When he was confident that the coast was clear, John scampered out and closed the door behind him, leaving the woozy man mumbling his profanities as though nothing had occurred. John hoped that lightheadedness would remain with this soldier in the coming battle.

The Rebel would, however, have the wherewithal to remember faintly hearing a strange voice from above. "Take care, general. I sincerely hope that your disposition improves with age." John had taken to the air once again, and he had come away with a greater appreciation for the sweet smell of a fresh breeze.

He was pleased; there was still plenty of time to return to the Garlach house before dawn, so he decided to swing around just a bit more to the east. What he discovered were even more Confederate encampments. His worst fears were realized.

A Rebel force of great concentration was settling in and around Gettysburg. If that detachment of Union cavalry to the west of town was worth its salt, it would detect the enemy's presence in the early morning, and initiate a frantic call up of the main body of Federal troops, wherever they were. With any luck, help would not be far off.

Unfortunately, all of this would take place in rapid succession while John was safe and secure once more under the Garlach's floorboards. That meant when he awoke at dusk, nearly a full day's worth of hard fighting would have already elapsed. He earnestly hoped that the Army of the Potomac was finally up to the task.

Praying for a Union victory was totally out of the question. If there were such a thing as a merciful God, would He have given his blessing for the creation of creatures like himself, or for the dissolution of the greatest government on earth? John reasoned that the answer to both questions was no.

Even as he reached the outskirts of Gettysburg just before dawn, all was quiet still. John returned to Baltimore Street; his rats, the darkness of the crawl space, and the cool, damp earth bed awaited him. His anxiety over the upcoming battle refused to slacken. As he finally drifted off to a much needed sleep, he could not help but ask himself what terrible carnage would await him on his native soil when the sun went down?

Chapter 15

The Perfect Soldier

As dusk slowly descended on the town, John opened his eyes once more to the annoying sound of loud banging, only this time, it was not his Cousin Henry's hammer; rather, the din was a deadly mix of rifle and artillery fire. The war had come to Gettysburg with a vengeance.

He listened intently to the mayhem as he snaked his way toward the wooden panel that faithfully kept his presence a secret. The streets within the town were bursting with shouts, curses, orders, sobs, pleas, and prayers. Hell itself could not have contained such a resounding intensity.

John's first thought was that the Army of the Potomac was badly beaten once again, perhaps as badly as at Chancellorsville, and had retreated with gusto through Gettysburg to escape being engulfed by the gray minions of General Lee. Those sad conclusions were not far off the mark. He scampered out from under the crawlspace without bothering to dust himself off.

He planned to hop the boundary fence, and then make his way back through the side alley to Baltimore Street to get a clearer picture of the situation, but his heightened sense of hearing detected a presence in the Garlach's shed. John walked towards it and opened the door inquisitively; he stepped inside and found a blue clad soldier hiding shamelessly under the cover of some cordwood near a trough of pig slop.

John identified himself as a friend, and told the terrified trooper that it would be safe to come out. When the man reluctantly complied and emerged from his sanctuary, John was disgusted to see from the uniform frock that this was no ordinary private, but rather, a full fledged Union general. No wonder the country was in peril, he thought, with cowards and skulkers the likes of these leading good, stout patriots in defense of the country.

John lost all control; he reached out and grabbed the general by the face in a claw like grip, flinging him unceremoniously backwards into the shed. "Stay there where you belong," he hissed, "trembling in the dark with no honor or loyalty. You have done enough damage for one day."

The sound of the general clattering over the woodpile brought a woman out the back door of the kitchen. John turned ever so slightly to his right and saw his Cousin Catherine approaching. Fortunately, she did not recognize him in the twilight, but he reasoned that he could no longer use the house as his primary resting place; the Garlachs' would be on guard now that their property had been violated.

Of even greater significance, this miserable excuse for a soldier had nearly brought about a horrific paradox. What if Catherine HAD gotten a good look at John? He thought of the terrible consequences, and his anger towards the faux soldier intensified. He thought briefly of killing him, sort of an addition by subtraction scenario for the Army of the Potomac, but there was not enough time.

John reached up and sprang over the fence before Catherine could get any closer. He hoped that she would also be disgusted with the general's conduct and refuse him a place of refuge, but deep down, he knew from personal experience that she was a kind soul who would refuse no one in time of trouble. The bastard would be well cared for.

He made his way along the side alleyway to the front of the house. A desperate scene of retreat presented itself when he began his walk along Baltimore Street towards the diamond in the center of town. All manner of equipment was strewn throughout —caissons, wagons, rifles, back packs, empty ammunition boxes; anything and everything one could imagine related to the art of war.

An occasional, desperate, wide eyed Union soldier would dart across to an adjoining side street, followed by a pack of howling Rebels in close pursuit. This was an indication to John that the Confederates had indeed won the day and taken possession of the entire town.

There were few civilians walking about the streets, and even fewer poking their heads out of the darkened house windows. The majority of the townsfolk were huddled in their cellars for safety from shot and shell. Those unfortunates with no basements were forced to lie flat on the floors of their homes, lest they be struck by a stray bullet or worse.

The conspicuous absence of locals scurrying around did prove to be a decided benefit for John in one way, since there would be fewer people about who could possibly bump into and identify him. But even if such an unfortunate incident did take place, he was sure that the person's credibility would be open to question due to the extreme circumstances brought on by the battle. It could simply be passed over as a case of mistaken identity during a highly stressful situation.

Surprisingly, the only locals John saw with any regularity were women busy flitting in and out of houses with all types of strange red flagging material. A closer inspection revealed that red shirts, skirts, towels, and scarves were being tacked on windows and doors to indicate that wounded men were being tended to inside.

The distrustful Rebels would rush in, search the houses for hidden Union stragglers, and then invariably apologize and file out when they were convinced of the temporary hospital's authenticity. John was stopped several times by hostile soldiers, but his civilian clothing was a good ruse to portray the image of a worried husband attempting to return to his wife and children cut off in another part of town.

To their credit, the Rebels showed compassion and let him pass in every instance. John concluded that although the secessionists were in the wrong, these men were not the vicious, marauding rabble that many Northern newspapers had made them out to be. Despite the fact that they were the invaders, John could not help noting their chivalrous attitude, and their sincere wishes that he would find his family safe from harm.

When he reached the diamond, John turned onto Chambersburg Street and passed the Eagle Hotel, which was now a bee hive of Rebel activity. He looked across the street and recognized Christ Lutheran Church, with its distinct, white Greek columns at the top of the entrance stairs, surrounded by sturdy brick walls, and a domed cupola complete with cross rising above its roof.

John stared at the cupola and then winced with fear and loathing, his hatred for the Redeemer now mixing equally with that for the Confederates. And yet, there was something in that scene that was very comforting to him, although he could not put his finger on just what it was. He inched his way closer to the church, despite the growing pain it caused him with every step he took.

It was then that an elderly matron hobbled by with a wicker basket filled with bed sheets. She noticed John staring at the church, and stopped to talk to him. "Please say that you are here to lend us some assistance," she asked hopefully.

"I…I don't understand what you mean," John stammered in honest confusion.

"Are you here to help us… inside that is, with all the wounded soldiers? They are in desperate need of comfort. The surgeons are doing the best that they can, but there are so many young men in dire straights. They die before our very eyes in the pews, calling out to God, their mothers, wives, and sweet hearts. It is all so horrible."

Her voice trailed off, and she lowered her head in despair. "I am sorry," John replied, but I must get back to my wife and children to see to their safety. We were separated, you see."

"Of course," she replied with heavy hearted approval. "I suppose a man's first duty IS to his family."

She paused, looked up at the head of the church stairs, and shook her head in disbelief. "Can you imagine the depravity of these Rebels? They shot Mr. Howell in cold blood, right there on the top step. Can they sink no lower?"

"Who is…who was…Mr. Howell?" John said with interest, correcting himself.

"He was the chaplain of the 90th Pennsylvania Infantry. He stayed here voluntarily with the injured from the regiment, to give them hope and reassurance that the Lord had not deserted them in their most desperate hour. For his service, he was shot down like a dog by a Rebel passing in the street. A finer man of God will never be found."

John looked up and saw blood still puddling and dripping on the stairs. THAT was the attraction he felt! He had a deep craving to climb the stairs and lap up the sweet remnants of the holy man, who received no help for his noble deeds from his so called Creator; but he dared not get any closer. The pain was excruciating.

He snickered shamelessly with a feeling of great satisfaction, and then laughed at the irony of the situation while his eyes radiated a sparkling crimson color. This reaction brought a look of horror on the old woman's face. "My God, you are MAD!" she exclaimed as she scampered up the stairs with her would be bandages. "Help! Someone please help me!"

When she reached the arched, white entrance door, a limping Union soldier with pistol in hand came hobbling from the church, ready to answer her call. She fell into his arms and turned around to point out and explain the reason for her outburst, but John was gone. Exhausted and bewildered, she crossed quickly herself and rushed screaming inside the church. The bewildered soldier followed close behind her, unwilling to leave his wounded friends.

John worked his way back towards the diamond. He wanted to assess the extent of the damage caused by the Rebels, but he was also hopeful that in all the confusion he might be lucky enough to encounter another gray clad field commander. It was only midnight, still plenty of time before dawn to disable another dog of war.

But Confederate forces grew as thick as green flies as he continued west. No longer able to walk the main streets without constant inquiries, he went down a dead end and took to the air to survey their positions. Looking back, he saw that the Rebels had indeed gained full control of the town, with the main line strung out as far as Middle Street, from the Hagerstown Pike past Rock Creek by the Hanover Road.

They were facing Union forces that had ultimately fallen back to good defensive positions along Culp's Hill, Cemetery Hill, Cemetery Ridge, and down towards Little Round Top, a place with a spacious view that John often frequented with his Fahnestock chums. The long blue line was developing the shape of an inverted fish hook, with the exception of a group of Federals atop Culp's Hill slightly to the east.

John muttered out loud with disdain. "At least they retreated well enough. I was afraid this group might have half a mind to keep going all the way to Washington. This means they intend to fight it out right here. Good! I was not schooled as a soldier, but if we stay put and let the Rebels come to us, I think we will give them a thrashing they will not soon forget. The question then becomes, will this General Lee somehow find a way to trick us yet again?"

John snapped out of his soliloquy, then turned and flew around to survey the Rebel lines to the west when he noticed a large group of Federal prisoners milling about like sheep near the grounds of Pennsylvania College. He toyed briefly with the idea of swooping down and attacking their guards in an effort to free them, but they were now situated too far behind enemy lines to link up with the rest of the Union army.

Besides, it would more than likely wind up a very messy affair that could not be accomplished without a multitude of witnesses, effectively destroying the most powerful tool of the night creature, the element of secrecy. Also, news of the incident would definitely focus the attention of the blasted Freemasons. They were indeed sprinkled throughout on both sides of the firing lines; he could smell them. No, his original plan would be followed to the letter.

The remaining Confederates to the west of town were spread out along Seminary Ridge, controlling the Hagerstown Road and the Cashtown Pike. John knew that he would be unable to attack any high ranking Rebels if they were bivouacked within the confines of the Lutheran Theological Seminary, for obvious reasons, so he chose to try his luck back at the Pike. It occurred to him that such a position would be an ideal location for a Rebel command headquarters.

Luck was with him, but only up to a point. There was indeed a great deal of activity, with much of it centered on the small, two story stone house occupied by Mrs. Mary Thompson, or more appropriately, the Widow Thompson, as she was known in town. John remembered her as a thin faced, rather plain looking woman, but she was courteous, and not one to pry into the business of others.

As he made his descent into the canopy of a large apple tree standing in the front yard about 50 feet from the house, he could see her arguing vehemently with several Rebel officers alongside her newly dismantled post and rail fencing that was being taken for the evening's firewood by the graybacks. She pointed her finger in a jabbing motion towards the missing fencing, then bobbed her head back and forth in a rage as she ripped into the Confederates; they stood rigid, tight lipped, and looked thoroughly miserable as a result of her severe dressing down.

John found it to be an extraordinarily odd scene, a lone old woman berating armed men of some degree of authority, with scores of enemy soldiers within a stone's throw. He surmised that it was only their ingrained Southern chivalry that prevented them from summarily ending the mostly one way conversation. They could hardly get a word in.

Just as the widow was beginning to pick up even more steam, another soldier emerged from the house and headed directly towards them. His presence seemed to buoy the spirits of the brow beaten officers, who would probably have preferred charging an artillery battery than being confronted by an irate female.

John listened attentively as the man gently introduced himself to her. The widow stood silent and drop jawed when she learned that she was in the presence of none other than General Robert E. Lee himself. But Mary was not the only one who was impressed. When John overheard the preliminary introduction, he too was taken aback, and he focused on the man to the exclusion of all else.

He was about six feet tall, in his early 50's perhaps, with piercing eyes and a kind face that was partially covered by a full, white beard. However, there seemed to be an air of propriety surrounding the manner in which he conducted himself. This was the prototype for the famed, knightly, soldier of the South, of that John was certain. Lee looked as though he was born to wear his military uniform.

John sincerely wished that Lee had taken Winfield Scott's earlier offer, which was to remain in the regular army and command the Union forces, rather than take up arms in defense of his home state of Virginia. If that particular scenario had played out the right way for the United States, John knew that he would have never been forced to abandon the safe confines of Etenel Babako.

He overheard the general patiently explain to the now sphinx-like Mary that her home was to be used as his temporary headquarters, but that she and her family would be allowed to remain in a separate portion of the house, with all due privacy afforded to them. He apologized to her for the destruction of her fence line, but stated that it was done out of necessity and not malice.

When he had finished, she snapped out of her reverie, thanking him profusely for his civility. With one final, dagger-filled glance aimed at the other officers, who either winced or looked uncomfortably away, she quickly disappeared into the house. The immediate domestic crisis was over. The officers relaxed at once and looked to their leader with gratitude; he said nothing further, but smiled for a brief moment in mild amusement at their predicament.

John was impressed with the commander's gracious and gratuitous explanations, under the circumstances; however, his heightened senses while he had been focusing on the man enabled him to detect something else that was startling, to say the least. Lee's heart beat was noticeably weak and out of synch. He was not near death, but there was no doubt that the stress of war was taking its toll.

John did not fool himself into believing that he could get close enough to this particular commander to enhance his already failing physical condition; there were too many soldiers and staff officers flitting about the general area. But he knew that he did not have to. The night creature's form slowly faded out until it disappeared from the branches of the apple tree. In its place, a thin cloud of reddish dust moved towards Lee as he dismissed his officers.

This was the time to strike! The cloud wafted down and settled gently around the great symbol of the South; the general swooned ever so slightly, and he brought an unsteady hand to his forehead as he blinked in an unsuccessful attempt to regain his equilibrium.

"You will bend to my will, general," a voice whispered with deep conviction. "The time will soon be ripe for a full frontal attack. Only this will bring you victory....remember."

The red dust moved off as a breeze took it effortlessly towards the direction of town. Lee shook his head and rubbed his eyes as an aide strode forward from the Widow Thompson's house with a look of concern on his face.

"General, are you all right, sir?"

"Yes...I...I'm fine now," Lee replied haltingly. "Thank you Major Taylor."

"Let's fix you up with a bite of food and something to drink, general. I'm sure there'll be something in the house."

The two soldiers turned and walked back to the scene of Lee's recent victory over the reluctant hostess. "Perhaps that would be a good idea; and please send for Major Marshall. I have some orders that need dictating, and they cannot wait."

John remained airborne while he made his way back to Gettysburg and the warehouse buildings stretched out along Railroad Street. There would be mountains of crates and cargo boxes to choose from for a safe and well deserved rest. His chief concern before he drifted off to sleep was how the Army of the Potomac would fare during the coming day.

Chapter 16

Two Quick Strikes

For the second consecutive evening, John awoke to the boom of artillery and the crackle of small arms fire. He rose from his crate that was situated in a remote, dark corner, and carefully removed the lid without a sound, mindful that the warehouse might not be completely vacant at this time.

John had chosen his resting place well. Confederate scavengers had already rifled through much of the warehouse looking for shoes, food, clothing, anything of possible value to an invading army on the move. He had foreseen this, so he hunkered down amid a number of crates marked "BIBLES," which ironically were left untouched by the Rebels once the contents of said crates were readily confirmed.

John thought it quite the irony that one of the "abandoned by God" was saved by the abandonment of the Almighty's own written word. He was personally disappointed that he had been unable to drink the chaplain's blood on the church steps the night before. It meant missing out on a tasty treat, so sleeping near a stack of bibles was a pleasant little blasphemy that he hoped he could duplicate at some future date.

Hearing neither voices nor movement of any kind in the building, he rose up and cocked his head toward the artillery barrage. It was to the south, and not within the town proper. That was good news, at least for the locals. Perhaps they had been spared the lion's share of the fighting after all.

John exited the warehouse onto Railroad Street, and then took to the air again, determined to find out what damage the Army of Northern Virginia had inflicted on the skittish Federals. A quick reconnaissance of Gettysburg Borough revealed surprisingly little physical damage to the town buildings, considering the circumstances. However, the flotsam and jetsam of war had been left behind for the dazed and frightened citizenry to deal with, and the industrious Rebels had barricaded many of the streets.

As John made his way south, the Union defensive line seemed to be nearly the same as it had been the night before, only a bit more ragged. The Confederate line was a poor duplicate, with tattered units on both ends. It looked as though the Yankees had repulsed fierce flank attacks near Little Round Top, the Devil's Den, and Culp's Hill, leaving thousands of dead and dying blue and butternut clad soldiers in the field.

The smell of blood and gore that came courtesy of the many casualties made John lightheaded and ravenous. He wanted to set down in the darkness, walk about, and take his pick of the litter, but there were other soldiers stumbling about, desperately trying to locate their missing comrades. Anyway, business before pleasure, Mr. Fahnestock always used to say.

The good news was that the Union lines had checked Lee's Invincibles, at least on this day. John wondered; could the Army of the Potomac have developed a backbone? Did its generals finally make the right decisions, or was fighting on U.S. soil an additional incentive? Whatever the reasons, the results were favorable, and John liked their chances in the morning if they maintained their positions, AND if Lee had no tricks hidden up his gray sleeve.

Just to make sure there were no new Confederate units lurking in the weeds waiting to strike, John decided to reverse direction and check back along the Chambersburg Pike, the road that so many secessionists had recently used with such fluidity.

He passed over Seminary Ridge, and shortly after that, McPherson's Ridge. Except for occasional small groups of riders, the pike did not seem to portend any significant danger. But when John hovered over Herr's Ridge about four miles out of town, he suddenly came upon a large encampment of Rebel troops just settling in for a good rest, their campfires dotting the landscape like so many fireflies lighting in the grass.

From the looks of them, they had not been engaged in any of the previous two days' actions; that made them all the more dangerous. Fresh reinforcements might have just enough strength to breach a weak spot in the Union line; and once that line was broken, the devil would come to supper. Was this the missing trump card that Lee had not yet drawn from the deck?

John decided that this particular camp might be his best bet to strike a resounding blow. He followed his previous modus operandi, and with the help of his faithful allies, stealth and darkness, he easily set down between the perimeter picket posts and the small tent village spread out on both sides of the pike.

Blending in among the Confederates was once again an easy task. Most of the men continued to wear whatever they pleased, or more accurately, whatever they could find. All John needed was a rifle and a hat, the latter having been left behind underneath the Garlachs house. Walking nonchalantly about the camp with an occasional nod or wave to passersby, he eventually came upon an unattended rifle and kepi by one of the tents.

Once he had them in his possession, his cheap disguise was complete. He felt compelled to hurry. If it was Lee's intention that this group was to take part in a clash tomorrow, the soldiers would certainly be up and on the move into position before dawn. He made his way towards the center of the encampment, passing clusters of soldiers plopped lazily around fires and tents while they wrote letters, played cards, or passed around bottles of O Be Joyful.

He suddenly found himself walking directly behind a well dressed officer with long, curly dark hair. However, that was not what brought him to John's attention. The man left the drifting scent of honeysuckle in his wake; for John, it brought back memories of the barber shop in York, and another thought that this soldier was perhaps a bit too dandified for his chosen profession.

Nevertheless, he followed him a short way to one of the larger tents, where other officers were lolling around a camp fire, drinking coffee and other spirits. John had hit the bull's eye. He drifted off to the side of the tent and squatted down on the ground to choose his next snack. The man he had followed seemed to be in command of these field officers, although he was much less formal than his previous two victims.

In fact, he had an almost happy go lucky air about him, along with the honeysuckle, and he was soon drinking from a silver flask that was being passed around the fire. He boasted about his "most beautiful Sallie," and soon waxed poetic while twisting his mustache, drawing pained expressions and sarcastic whispers from his amused audience.

But there was one officer in the group who was not amused. In fact, he had suddenly ignored the professions of undying affection, and was staring grim faced in the direction of the stranger sitting by the tent. John's predatory instinct instantly switched to one of survival as the officer excused himself from the group, got up and started slowly towards him. "Hurry back, Lo," one of the officers cried out. "George is just getting warmed up."

A Freemason was approaching! John began to pick up the faint scent of rotting meat. He rose up and began to walk stiffly away from the campfires, fighting the screaming urge to take to the night sky in full flight.

He did not have to turn around to know that the officer was following him at a respectable distance, but was closing fast. John also began to feel unclean, indicating that a crucifix was somewhere nearby. It was a safe bet that his pursuer had one in his possession. John picked up the pace until he entered an isolated wooded area where soldiers and the light from their fires ceased to be a hindrance.

He slipped nimbly behind a large oak and waited breathlessly for his pursuer. When the man had nearly passed the tree, he stopped and pulled a small cross from his breast pocket; he held it out in front of him and spoke to the darkness. "I know what you are, FILTH. SHOW YOURSELF IN THE NAME OF GOD."

John immediately stepped out and fixed his gaze into the eyes of the startled officer, who was not expecting such a quick or close encounter. The predator was now the prey, frozen in fear. "As you have commanded, sir," John snarled in a mock reply.

With the possibility of sounding the alarm eliminated, John deftly covered the crucifix with his kepi, threw them both far off into the woods, and slammed the officer unceremoniously to the ground. It was then that he got his first good look at his adversary. He was middle aged, balding, but had a full beard and sparkling, mischievous eyes.

"How did you know?" John whispered to the prostrate form beneath him. "What gave me away?" The disabled man replied haltingly, unable to rouse himself from his hypnotic state. "Your eyes...in the...firelight...bright red."

John wasted no time and drained as much blood as he dared, pulling the soldier's lapel back over the wound when he had finished. He would have very much preferred ripping this natural enemy to shreds, but he had bigger fish to fry, and there might be other Freemasons about who could take this murder as a sign that a greater enemy than the Yankees was out and about.

The man would awake in a few minutes, believing that he had simply fainted. By the time that occurred, John was long gone. He had been unable to hit his intended mark, that sweet smelling dandy, but he hoped that it would prove to be a successful operation nonetheless. The officer was, from the look of his uniform, a brigadier general. Perhaps the man would lead his men to their deaths in some futile, desperate charge. He could only hope.

John made his way south behind the enemy lines that opposed the inverted Union fish hook. The Confederates were stretched out from the Hagerstown Road to both Round Tops. He flew from camp to camp, trying to find another officer whose decision might end the lives of countless fellow secessionists.

Just when John thought that he had run out of time, he found himself over a peach orchard off the Emmitsburg Road. A Rebel brigade was stationed nearby; but what made the scene interesting was a small group of riders, one of whom seemed to exude authority and self confidence.

John followed them over Warfield Ridge to the Flaherty Farm on the Millerstown Road; he was quite happy with this turn of events. John never cared much for old man Flaherty; he was a miserable excuse for a farmer and possessed a nasty disposition on top of that. Having him thrown out of his own house was a charming thought. By now, John knew a field headquarters when he saw one.

Having chosen his second general of the night, the next step was gaining entry into the farmhouse to complete his task, despite lacking a proper invitation, so to speak. John decided to pretend using his knowledge of Gettysburg and the area as the means to achieve his ends. He walked tentatively towards two pickets stationed about 70 yards away.

"That's far enough," one soldier's voice boomed. "State yur bizniss and be quick about it, else I'll blow yur damned head off."

"I have come to see the general," John replied weakly. "I have some information that he might find useful."

The two men eyed him up and down suspiciously, then whispered among themselves as they searched him for weapons. Finally, one of them gestured him on with his rifle.

"All right, yung' feller. You can sees the genral, but if'n he don't like what he hears, reckon I'll still git to blow yur head off. This a way."

John took the lead and walked straight ahead, with the barrel of the soldier's rifle occasionally sticking in his back. When they reached the farmhouse, passed the sentries and started the climb up the stairs, a junior officer emerged from the front door and stood in their path.

"What have we got here, Corporal Hanson, a spy?"

"Can't say fur sure, major. He sez he's got big news for Old Pete."

"That's right," John interjected. "I've come from the Emmitsburg Road, and there are some things he should know."

The road name mentioned intrigued the young officer. He had thoughts that perhaps there might be Federals coming up that way around to flank their lines; this stranger might prove useful, but he was still wary. "And why should I believe YOU, my young YANKEE friend?"

"Because I am no friend of the Yankees," John answered. "I WAS originally from this area of Pennsylvania, but moved just outside of Baton Rouge years ago. My loyalties lie with–Jefferson Davis, God bless him, and the Confederacy, sir."

"We shall see about that right now; follow me." The officer opened the door and they stepped inside. Sitting at a table pouring over a series of maps was a big, full bearded, bear of a man who filled up his gray uniform quite impressively.

"I'll draw a gallon out of this bird," John whispered to himself, "if only I could get him under the right circumstances."

"General, this man says that he has some information for you. Considering the service that Harrison has done for you thus far, he may be worth listening to."

The general nodded in agreement, and then looked John over pensively; he took his unlit cigar out of his mouth and let out a sigh. "Well, out with it, man. What is so important that you have come here in the middle of the night?"

"I would very much prefer to speak with you alone, general," John said respectfully. He looked fearfully over at the junior officer. "I have taken a great personal risk in coming here, and the fewer sets of ears the better, if you catch my drift."

The general blinked as if in thought and then replied. "Major Sorrel, if you would kindly excuse us for a moment."

"Yes, sir, general," the officer countered as he saluted and left the house, closing the door behind him. He shot John a final stare. "I'll be right outside."

The general shifted in his chair. "My name is Longstreet; you have my attention, sir. Who are you and what is it that you wish to tell me that simply cannot wait?"

Longstreet!! John had hit the mother load. He remembered the name from the many newspaper articles he had read reporting the war. Lee relied heavily on this soldier for advice and results in the field. John looked around the room and saw that the windows were shuttered closed. When he returned his gaze towards the general, red beads of fire pierced the man's eyes, rooting him to his chair.

"I'm here to make a withdrawal from your personal account, general," John countered blithely. He quickly moved around the table and positioned himself behind the man, bending down and making an innocuous bite in his neck. After several minutes, he stood up and wiped his mouth while turning up the man's gray lapel.

"General, I must say, of all my recent victims, you are the tastiest, AND the most satisfying. You are to be congratulated." John waited until his mark had begun to regain consciousness, then he gazed at him once more. The general got up slowly, looked a bit confused, and ushered John to the door. When it was opened, the major and the sentry quickly reappeared.

"This man has nothing of consequence for us. Let him go," the general said blinking tentatively.

The major was concerned. "Are you all right, sir? You look piqued."

"Yes, yes, I'm fine, Moxley; just need a little sleep. Thank you."

With that, the picket was ordered to escort John back to his post and send him on his way. "Sorry I didn't git to blow yur head off, Yank; maybe some other time."

John was less than thrilled with this cretin. He had half a mind to snap the Reb in half when he reached the picket post, but his mission was accomplished. It was time to get some rest. He made his way to the Pitzer farm not far away, and dove under a straw pile in the barn's hayloft. It was not quite as secure as the warehouse on Railroad Street, but acceptable under short notice.

John thought long and hard; he had accomplished more than he dared imagine. Over the last three nights, he had stricken five high ranking Confederate officers. But would that be enough to help turn the tide in the Army of the Potomac's favor? The Federals, at least in this theater of operation, had precious little to crow about of late. He would have to wait for the following evening to answer his own question.

Chapter 17

The Butcher's Yard

John awoke to the sound of silence; this new development took him totally off guard. Unsure of the consequences, he rose slowly from the hay and strained his ears for the din of battle, but there was nothing to be heard. He brushed himself off with very little enthusiasm, and then crept to the hayloft door to sneak a peek outside.

What could have happened, he thought to himself. The two armies had been locked in bitter combat for two days, with the stage set for what looked to be a grand finale while he lay sleeping in the barn. Did that actually take place or not?

His mind immediately conjured up a worst case scenario. Lee had once again devised some brilliant battle plan that caught the Federal officers and men completely flatfooted. They panicked en masse after their lines were breached, and then the Army of Northern Virginia followed right behind and destroyed the Yankees piecemeal during the rout.

If the Union army in the east had ceased to exist, European intervention would soon follow, along with public pressure in the North for peace talks before the Rebels swarmed into Washington like angry, stinging wasps. John wondered if his plan was really a foolish dream in disguise, or if his venture into the war was just a classic example of too little and too late.

In either case, he had to uncover the truth. He waited for several agonizing hours for the cover of total darkness, then took swift flight due east, toward the previous day's lines of battle. When he passed over Warfield Ridge, a thick smell of blood filled the air and bathed his nostrils. There had been a great battle after all; as to its location, he simply had to follow his nose, which beckoned him with the reek of decay to veer slightly to the north, and Seminary Ridge.

As he closed in on the Emmitsburg Road, John made good use of his keen eyes. He peered through the darkness, and the sight was beyond even his comprehension. Thousands of dead and dying soldiers littered the ground, from the safety of the Rebel lines in the woods, all the way to Cemetery Ridge. One side had made a glorious but near suicidal charge in what seemed like an effort to pierce the other's lines, just as John had surmised.

The question was: WHICH side had been slaughtered? He circled cautiously, then focused on a spot where there was a large concentration of bodies along the Emmitsburg Road. Touching the ground lightly, the scent of rotting flesh, blood, and internal organs mixed in with the soil to make an undeniably surreal ghoulish brew. He could not walk three paces without stepping on a body, or at least parts of one.

Despite the carnage, John experienced a deep feeling of relief. The ravaged soldiers were in fact Confederates. True to their code, they had taken the initiative, charging the strong defensive lines of the entrenched Federals, and consequently paid a heavy price.

His mind raced back to the previous 48 hours. On the first day, the Rebels had nearly routed the Army of the Potomac, sending it scurrying unceremoniously through Gettysburg until it reorganized and held a position on Cemetery Ridge. At the time, secesh generals and soldiers alike must have been exhilarated, feeling that this was perhaps the start of another Chancellorsville episode.

On the second day, the ends of the Union fishhook line were severely tested. Lee must have been trying to roll up either the shank or the barb; only this time, the defensive minded Federals stood firm under the relentless pressure. The Confederate's previous day's euphoria possibly began to lose steam in the reality of bitter fighting with a well entrenched enemy.

Finally, the third day witnessed an almost unbelievable charge over several hundred yards of open field, like some huge, gray wave attempting to crash over a blue rocked bulkhead. Perhaps after pummeling both flanks without success, Lee may have come to the conclusion that the Yankees were strung out so far that their soft spot was directly in the center of their line! Splitting that line would have resulted in the victory on United States soil that the South and its waffling European allies had been waiting for.

But then again, perhaps John's "suggestion" to Lee at the Thompson House festered to the point where the great general could no longer resist the subliminal urge to strike a decisive blow. Whatever the reason, it was a mistake of enormous magnitude; Lee would have to shoulder the blame for it, while his army would have to suffer the consequences.

And what consequences they were. John stood with his hands on his hips and completed a 180 degree turn. The still, bloated bodies of the dead, and the writhing, twitching, prostrate forms of the wounded screaming hoarsely in pain were intermingled everywhere. The Confederates lying at John's feet looked as though they had been butchered, but that had taken place during the day; it was now well into the evening hours.

Why hadn't a cease fire been agreed to so that the wounded could be removed and properly attended to? While there were individual soldiers scattered throughout the field braving random gunfire to search for their comrades in arms, the vast majority of injured Rebels were left, temporarily at least, to the mercy of their God. "Good luck to that," John mumbled.

His mouth puckered in disgust at the very thought of it. Yes, here was the will of God in all its glory and divine majesty, a slaughterhouse scene of unimaginable proportions. Only His assent could have allowed the pure evil loose in the world to manifest itself in such intensity. John thought back to the words of Satan himself: "All this I will give you, if you will but kneel down and worship me."

The devil WAS certainly dancing a merry jig this night. A panoramic view displayed one ghastly scene after another. A glance to John's left showed a group of 10 men blown apart by an artillery shell. Arms, legs, and even heads were peppered liberally around the bloody torsos.

A look ahead revealed several soldiers who were killed by pieces of exploded post and rail fencing that had been lined along the road. One man had a large chunk of railing blown straight through his neck. He had grabbed both bloody ends with his hands, as if in a futile effort to dislodge it. He died with his blackened tongue sticking out, while flies buzzed about happily laying their eggs in his gaping mouth.

The other soldier was quite young. John guessed that he was no more than 15 years old. An artillery shell had blown the post in half, leaving a dangerous spike in the ground at a 45 degree angle. During the billowing smoke and confusion of the charge, this unfortunate boy had run right into it, and he became impaled all the way through to his back pack.

His arms and legs hung stiffly at his side. His face betrayed an expression of utter amazement, with his eyes staring wildly at the ground, while his mouth was contorted, as though still trying to scream for help above the din of battle. No one had heard him, or even taken notice. A glance to the right showed one man shot through the side of the mouth; he was kneeling and still trying to staunch the bleeding, to no avail.

Another soldier had the top half of his head blown clean off; his brains were missing. A third man lay frozen in a sitting position, propped up against a gutted horse. His left foot had been shot off, and he had tried desperately to apply a belt tourniquet before finally blacking out and bleeding to death. The belt was still in his hands. Perhaps all that he needed was 30 more seconds of consciousness.

If all this was not enough, the wounded that had been left behind groaned, shrieked, pleaded, prayed, and twitched about in a hideous, agonizing Greek chorus. John returned to thoughts of his childhood Sunday bible classes and his kindly old instructor, Michael Clark, a man who did not believe in the adage "Spare the rod and spoil the child."

Surely even he would have agreed that the horrendous sounds in the aftermath of this bloody battlefield would have eclipsed the maddening voices heard during the telling of one of his favorite stories, the affront to God that was the Tower of Babel.

A strange sensation overcame John the more he gazed over the carnage; one that he did not even realize was taking place. His initial hatred towards these Confederates, and his joy in their defeat, was replaced ever so slightly with pity and respect.

They were still trying to destroy the best country on earth; John was adamant about that fact. But perhaps they felt that they had been wronged, or worse, felt that they were defending their own particular freedoms, not to mention the future of their homes and families. For whatever action John was going to take in the future to preserve the Union, it would no longer be fueled by hate.

Despite the feelings of waste and shame felt by the survivors on every battlefield after the firing has stopped, the sporadic displays of humanity and compassion were still in evidence. Wounded men were dragged or carried toward the Rebel lines on Seminary Ridge by loyal comrades who thought more for their friends' welfare than their own, considering the deadly accuracy of the Federal sharpshooters, even in the dark.

The searchers could have stayed safely in the woods and gotten a few precious hours of sleep to renew their spent minds and bodies, but that was gladly shunned aside. John watched them in fascination as they ventured out to the locations where they recalled their campmates being shot to pieces in that mind numbing charge.

His thoughts were suddenly interrupted by the sound of a slow, sorrowful voice from behind. "You lookin' fer someone in Pettigew's division, friend? I come upon em' over thataway." John turned slightly to see a tattered, tired looking soldier pointing to his left while he tiptoed respectfully among the corpses.

"I'm a searchin' for mah brother. We wuz side by side when the Yankee artillery raked our lines by that damned fence. It slowed us up severely. You seen a boy in yur travels?" The man's voice began to trail off. "He's only 15, so I promised ma I'd.... kinda look after im'."

John closed his eyes, bowed his head for a moment, and then replied haltingly; "Keep going the way you are now." The soldier perked up at the news. "Have ya seen im'? Is he wounded? Is he hurt bad?"

John turned his back to the man and moved away, uncomfortable with the thought of being the bearer of such bad tidings. "Just…keep going. You'll find him soon enough." The eager soldier picked up his pace and disappeared with renewed hope into the darkness.

However, there was one lone forager in the distance moving toward the Union lines who caught John's eye. For one thing, he acted as though he were completely oblivious to the prospect of being shot to pieces; the man moved about slowly and deliberately without even looking up to measure his distance to Cemetery Ridge. For another, he seemed to linger over each wounded man that he came upon, after which the soldier would cease his cries and movements altogether.

Something was not quite right. He dressed the part of a Rebel soldier, but he was without pack, rifle, or litter. John's curiosity got the better of him; he made his way towards this man, who was standing with his back to him as he made his approach. When he got to within a few short yards, John stopped dead in his tracks, almost as though his feet had become stuck in a bog. A swift, overwhelming feeling of dread washed over him, no mean feat considering the fact that he had by now fully harnessed the impressive powers of his altered state. This dread brought about an immediate understanding of just who he was about to confront.

Chapter 18

A Conversation with Death

The mysterious figure turned slowly around as John made his approach. He certainly looked the part of an ordinary Rebel soldier; homespun, ragged clothing hung loosely off his thin frame, while his everyman face sported a scruffy beard, right down to his unflattering brown eyes. But the image portrayed was anything but the truth.

In his stone cold heart, John knew that he was the weaker of the two. He addressed the figure with some small measure of sarcasm mixed lightly with contempt, although much of it was false bravado, and much akin to whistling past the graveyard. This was not a being to trifle with.

"So, my dear Death, you have come to take full advantage of this grisly scene and reap a rich harvest tonight. You must pardon my interruption." John bowed slowly to complete his mocking salutation.

"Please, do not keep your future subjects waiting on my account." John spread out his arms in a sweeping gesture. "Choose whomever strikes your fancy; drag them kicking and screaming into the blackness of the abyss. There is no one to challenge you."

The figure looked forlornly at John, shook his head slowly from side to side, and let out a single, mournful sigh before speaking. "Even beings such as you do not understand my motives...or my purpose. But then again, it has been that way since the dawn of time, and will remain that way till crack of doom."

John was thrown completely off guard by the reply. "Why ELSE can you be here, except to rob these brave men of their life force?"

The reply was soft and thoughtful. "I need not steal what they are about to forfeit by the unnatural acts of war. On the contrary, I am here to end their suffering, and to open the door for them. Attend me."

Death walked over to a splayed out soldier who was laying face up, moaning in agony from a shell fragment that had nearly eviscerated him; he bent down on one knee and gently took the Rebel by the hand. The moaning gradually grew faint, and then soon stopped altogether; the soldier slowly closed his eyes, very much like a child who had finally lost the strength to fight an oncoming night's sleep.

No sooner had that soldier passed on, another cried out for his wife in the darkness. A closer inspection revealed that this Confederate had been shot by mini balls in the groin and upper chest. He appeared to be in his 20's. The once handsome young man was gurgling blood from his mouth, while his body jerked involuntarily in spasms of intense suffering.

A cool hand on the soldier's hot forehead, followed by a gentle stroking of his hair, produced a calmness that only sheer exhaustion could bring. After several long, deep breaths, all pain and movement was gone.

Now it was John's turn to be taunted; Death stood erect and leveled his own accusations. "Many brave men have need of me this night. There is much work to be done, and precious little time. But why are YOU here, NIGHT CREATURE? Have you come for a bountiful feast yourself? The market place is open and well stocked for your feed, I assure you. You will want for nothing."

John turned away in an effort to mask his surprise and anger, and then gazed in the direction of the Rebel lines before making his retort.

"You must know why I am here. What secret on this earth can be kept from a being the likes of you? I have a higher purpose than merely gorging on these mortals."

"Yeees," Death replied. "You have taken it upon yourself to challenge the destiny of half a continent. Such a course of action has not gone unnoticed, and not just by me."

John's eyes widened; his plan was still in its infancy. He could not imagine that it had attracted so much attention this quickly. That could mean only one thing.

Death continued; "The Council of Djadadjii has already deemed your actions as a violation of The Covenant. It would be wise for you to make yourself scarce, lest they do it for you."

John paused for a moment to collect his thoughts; he had been warned, which was a luxury that most transgressors never received, and he was genuinely grateful. He tried to steer the conversation on to more common ground, albeit ever so briefly, but the cries and shrieks of the dying brought them back to the reality of the killing field before them.

John finally gave up. "It would seem that time is a precious commodity for the both of us this night. Perhaps it would be best for all concerned if we were to go our separate ways."

A long silence followed, one that seemed to build in intensity as the seconds ticked away. Finally, Death broke the stillness of the moment.

"There is an old saying: Every man to his fate, for good or ill; YOUR work has increased MINE a thousand fold, but it is not my place to judge what is to be."

"Yes, for good or ill," John replied, inwardly pleased by the revelation that his recent actions had contributed to the Army of the Potomac's gruesome success. "Farewell."

With that, John took to the air without waiting for a reply. The thin, ragged figure watched without expression as John disappeared into the darkness toward Spangler's Woods, then he lowered his head and continued his systematic tour of the carnage laid out before him. He shook his head sadly; so many needed his help.

John made an hour long sweep of the enemy positions. The Confederate forces that had been stationed in the town proper were withdrawn completely and subsequently re-deployed to bolster the two mile plus gray line along Seminary and Oak Ridges, stretching from the Emmitsburg to the Mummasburg Roads.

He felt that this signaled an important development. It looked as though the Rebels were reorganizing their lines in anticipation of repelling a FEDERAL attack this time. Perhaps the grand charge of yesterday had significantly drained their manpower. He certainly hoped this was the case, but there was one way to find out for sure.

Lighting down in the woods near Willoughby's Run south of the Chambersburg Pike, John melted in amongst the scores of secessionist soldiers bivouacked in the area. He picked up a discarded pack and swung it over his shoulder, then filched a Springfield musket and carried it loosely in one hand as he made his way slowly through throngs of grim faced Rebels. They were sitting and lying on the ground, some staring into space like mesmerized moths near a flame.

The conversations were revealing, yet puzzling to John at the same time. Many soldiers were dispirited and broken by the events of the day before, almost stunned by the horrific damage done to the Army of

Northern Virginia. Others spoke optimistically, hoping to get another opportunity to crack the Yankee lines and send them skedaddlin'.

But whether the men felt high or low, the overwhelming sentiments among the rank and file was that as long as General Lee was in command, he would find a way to lead them to victory, whatever the odds. A chilling thought came to John; this war was not going to end any time soon. Americans were fighting Americans, the best against the best.

John continued mulling over all of the Rebels' comments and opinions in his head, trying to get a better grip on the overall morale of their army, when he began to hear the sounds of battle once again. This time, it was not the din of rifle and artillery fire, but rather, the screams and moans of the wounded.

A short walk brought him to a scene of controlled carnage. John had stumbled into the middle of a Confederate military field hospital. If he thought the open field split by the Emmitsburg Road was appalling, the sights, sounds, and smells of this "haven" rivaled it in horror. It's lone saving grace was a natural spring that provided the doctors and wounded alike with fresh water.

As he went by one tent, a makeshift operating table had been set up with planking and barrels. An exhausted looking doctor wearing a blood stained apron was cutting off the leg of one poor soldier with what looked like an ordinary hacksaw, while orderlies held the flailing man down until the deed was done. His high pitched screams of agony were enough to raise the hairs on the back of a man's neck.

Conversely, there were also silent unfortunates with severe head wounds judged to be inoperable. They were stacked alongside one another like cordwood, well off to the side and out of the way, until their ends came quietly and without notice. At least many of them were not conscious enough to comprehend their dire condition, or their complete abandonment.

As John rounded a corner to escape the stench of pus and gangrene, he came upon a group of soldiers recovering from their recent encounters with the surgeons. Most of them had endured amputations, with only dirty, bandaged stumps to show for their patriotism.

The ultimate indignity was but a few yards away; they all had a clear view of a small mountain of their mangled arms and legs waiting to be carted off and unceremoniously buried. Their faces were etched with throbbing pain and despair.

It was not hard to discern their thoughts. How would they be able to provide for their wives and children, even if they were fortunate enough to make it back home alive? Most were dirt farmers who had barely subsisted before the war. Now they would be invalids for the rest of their lives, able to perform only the most menial of tasks, while the upper crust fire eaters who brought on this war remained safely in their homes spouting the same inflammatory rhetoric to anyone who was still disposed to listen.

John had witnessed enough. It was time to check on conditions of his own people within the town. Venturing between the encampments and picket posts, he took to the air for a short time until he reached Gettysburg. Even though the Rebs had vacated just a few scant hours before, a small number of the frightened residents were beginning to emerge from their homes and cellars to assess the damages.

It appeared that the chivalrous General Lee had made a point not to target the town's infrastructure or its civilian population, although there was no way of knowing just how many locals had perished. The crude barricades that had been piled up across the roads by the

Confederates could be removed with a bit of sweat equity, but it was surprising how well the town's buildings had fared over the course of the intense, three day battle.

At first glance, it was a safe assumption that civilian casualties were minimal. As John watched over the state of town affairs while flitting from rooftop to rooftop, residents would walk by occasionally with stunned Rebel prisoners. Those soldiers had somehow gotten left behind in the confusion of the silent pull out from the streets and houses. He thought it fortunate that the Confederates had treated the civilians well during their captivity; otherwise, there might have been some serious retribution. Stout Pennsylvanians were not to be trifled with.

Federals who had been in hiding since the retreat to Cemetery Ridge also had emerged. They were very relieved to be free once again, many of them hugging and thanking their civilian "hosts" profusely. John recognized the Union general whom he had discovered cringing in the Garlach's woodshed. "Too, too bad," he said ruefully to himself. "That officer would have better served his country dead."

Confident that the Army of the Potomac had taken Lee's best shot, and given as much in return, John thought it best to make his way back to his warehouse refuge. It would soon be daylight. He fully expected another clash to be winding down the following evening; its result would determine his next course of action.

In any event, it was well past midnight, and he knew that he would need to think about feeding before too long. Just as he was about to take flight, he overheard some of the townspeople in the street remark that their deliverance from the Rebels would make this the best Fourth of July celebration that they could ever have. It was at that very moment John came to the realization that it was in fact Independence Day.

Chapter 19

Algernon's Fateful Error

The sun was beginning to set when the dozen blue clad horsemen charged noisily up the River Road with sabers waving and guns firing. They engaged in mock cavalry clashes against one another, while throwing in a poor, mock rendition of the Rebel yell at the top of their lungs. There was, of course, the obligatory pause to resume their drinking. They had become accustomed to the watered down swill sold in the suttlers stores, so the strong Tennessee whiskey was beginning to take a heavy toll.

The Yankees were ecstatic, and determined to vent their enthusiasm in any shape or form. The lead horseman trotted up to the entrance path of Etenel Babako, wheeled about and sounded the charge; he galloped headlong toward the mansion with his saber tilted forward. The rest of the troop followed in short order, darting around the live oaks, and occasionally hacking away at the trunks and lower branches.

The startled Negroes tending the front orchards were frightened by the sight and sounds. They knew enough of human nature to realize that drunken men with weapons would have no second thoughts of firing upon darkies, so they dropped their pruning tools and rushed headlong toward the slave quarters.

Algernon heard the din from the overseer's office, and quickly made his way to the front of the mansion just as the lead horseman arrived. He scowled and stood his ground defiantly with his hands on his hips as the remaining soldiers rode up.

"We have no need of your services today, gentlemen; thank you," Algernon bellowed with his usual sarcasm. Union troops were no strangers to Etenel Babako by this time; the plantation was visited regularly to monitor the goings on.

"The PROPER military authorities were here just last week, and it was determined at that time that all was well. You are therefore trespassing on private property and will leave at once, or I will have you all reported." He looked at them with unabashed disdain, and then continued.

"I surmise from your present conditions that you have ventured from New Orleans, and are now headed back to your posts at Baton Rouge. I suggest that you finish the last leg of your journey post haste, before you get into serious trouble. Do I make myself clear.....gentlemen?"

Silence followed. One of the troopers got down from his horse and made his way unsteadily toward Algernon, eventually stopping within a few feet of him. "We are in no great hurry to return to the city, overseer." He turned and waved his hand behind him. "The lot of us are on French leave. You know what that is, don't you, you Cajun scum?"

"No, I do not," Algernon replied evenly as he tried to control his rising anger, "but from the sound of it, I suspect that in the end, there will be a dark, cozy guardhouse waiting patiently for you." He continued on. "But look on the bright side; you will have ample opportunity to sober up on government time, although I daresay that you will smell worse than you do now, as hard as that is to imagine."

The remaining mounted troopers laughed at the dressing down of their group leader, who could only blink and stand with his mouth open while he swayed back and forth in a serious battle of his own to remain upright. It was way too much information for him to process in his present condition. Finally, the speech settled in, along with the embarrassment of being whittled down in the presence of his comrades; the soldier rallied and regained some of his previous swagger.

"I'll bet a smart ass like you don't even know why we're all celebratin'.....but then again, maybe you do. Ain't you happy at the news?" The attitude of the soldiers changed rapidly despite their stupor. They stared at Algernon with suspicion, and leaned forward in their saddles to re-assess the situation.

"And what good news might that be, my inebriated Hector?"

"Why, Genral Ulyssees SSSS Grant, God bless im', has taken Vicksburg! It came through on the telegraph wire. The city surrendered uncun...uncondi....completely, and my name's Brenner." He beamed with joy at the very thought of it, and continued rambling on. "The big river, the Mississippi, it's ours now, to use as we damn well please, and you don't hafta be no flamin' Napoleon ta know the Confederacy's cut in two. Whatcha got ta say bout that choice tidbit, Reb?"

All eyes were now centered squarely on Algernon. He did not realize that the alcohol was letting this situation get out of hand; his response would be instrumental in defusing the growing tension. But he had grown too used to dealing with defenseless slaves. His pride and arrogance would prove to be his undoing, but then again, he always felt more powerful when his master was about to rise.

"My one and only concern is the proper running of this plantation, and I am the HEAD overseer. I have no time or inclination to bother with outside trifles. Besides, Jacques Dumaine, the owner of Etenel Babako, has already taken your silly Oath of Allegiance, so be gone. I have important matters to attend to."

"SILLY, you say," the soldier barked menacingly. "I spose you didn't bother with the Fourth of July neither, did you, REB? Now that I comes tu think of it, a patriot would have the Stars n' Stripes flyin' in honor of Independence Day, but I ain't seen it anywhere on the ways in, and I don't sees it on that blasted castle behind you, neither."

The troopers shook their heads in agreement. Several of them tugged lightly at the reigns of their horses and began to fan out slowly on either side of the mansion. Algernon saw that he was being flanked, but there was nothing he could do about it except stand his ground with a show of defiance and wait for the sun to disappear from view. It was going on 7PM.

The earlier shouts and woops from the road were an indication to him that there could be the possibility of some trouble, so he had stuffed a Colt revolver half way down the front of his pants prior to leaving the office. He made sure that the handle was in plain sight, but the Federals had strength in numbers.

Still, his master would be up and about any minute; then the pendulum of power would swing radically. He could not help himself. "I will not tell you again to leave the premises. If you do not go, you will surely suffer, in ways more horrible than you could ever imagine."

The lead horseman laughed hysterically in a high pitched tone. "Whatchoo gonna do..... report us? We're already in the soup for takin' off without so much as a bye yur leave from the colonel. But maybe, juuus' maybe, we can git back in Dutch by lettin' im' know that this here place is a nest o' Rebels, and that the Oath taken here by yur high n' mighty planter boss was nuthin' but a low down, dirty trick. That oughta get him thrown in jail, and this place taken over by the rightful U.S. government…that is, if'n we don't burn it first, o' course."

THAT WILL BE ENOUGH!" a deep, ominous voice boomed as if from on high; each drunkard jerked his head up to the center of the second floor balcony. Jacques Dumaine stood gripping the top of the iron railing in a sputtering rage. He was trying desperately to control his rising emotions; only Algernon noticed that the railing was beginning to bend in his hands.

"There will be no arrests, and certainly no burnings. I have been cleared personally by your Colonel Harrington. Now leave us. I want nothing more than to run my plantation in peace."

"Yur a goddamned liar!" one of the mounted soldiers shouted back at Dumaine. "Boys, this bastard's runnin' the place like nothin's goin' on at all. Good men are dyin' to save the Union, but he don't give a shit. And if the Rebs win, I'll bet he's got enuff gold in that house o' his to turn some heads the other way. Ain't that right, mister high and mighty?"

"I will not tell you again to leave," Dumaine hissed. "You cannot know the danger that you are in."

"WE'RE not in danger, old man; YOU are. But if you give us some o' that gold, we might decide to do a bye your leave after all. I think we'll take us a gander inside. When we git what we want, you'll git what you want. What say, boys?"

There was a resounding yes from the group; almost as if on cue, the troopers began to dismount from their horses. Algernon could stand the insolence no longer. He pulled the revolver from his belt and shot the soldier closest to him in the side of the head before Dumaine could order him to stop.

The skull literally exploded, showering brains and bone on the dead man's horse, which reared wildly in the air and galloped off behind the mansion. The groups' leader was momentarily stunned, but he recovered quickly and turned to his mount to retrieve a carbine from his saddle holster.

"YOU CAJUN BASTARD!" he screamed. "You killed Joe Wray, an' now I'm gonna kill you." The carbine never did leave the saddle holster. Algernon pumped three bullets into his back; the last one severed the man's spine. He flew against his horse from the momentum, and then dropped in a heap like a sack of potatoes, dead before he reached the ground.

Four of the drunken troopers waved their pistols at the overseer and fired; surprisingly, all four hit their target. Algernon was shot in the face, neck, stomach, and left forearm. The force of the bullets sent him backpedaling towards the porch of the mansion in a wide spray of blood; then he wheeled about and fell face down in the dust of the main pathway, the smoking Colt still in his hand.

There was a momentary pause while the gun smoke billowed about, and then one of the soldier brayed: "Let's burn her to the ground, boys." There was not even enough time for any of his comrades to answer. Dumaine sprang from the balcony with an unearthly howl and landed on the closest trooper, toppling him from his horse; he grabbed the man's head in his hands and jerked it violently. The neck snapped like a stalk of celery.

A rider behind Dumaine fired his revolver at point blank range into his back, but there was no effect. That shot was followed by two dozen others; some missed their marks, some found them. The wild, animal like features of Dumaine convinced the terrified soldiers that their collective efforts would inexplicably be in vain. Their only recourse was to put as much distance as they could between themselves and that.....thing! The nine remaining troopers swung their horses around and made a desperate dash for the safety of the River Road.

Dumaine was able to yank one last soldier from his horse as he attempted to make his escape. He sunk his teeth into the man's throat and ripped it to pieces, but his savagery was observed by the others as they rode away. Their abject terror convinced each man that this Jacques Dumaine was either stark raving mad...or much worse. They needed to return in greater numbers.

Dumaine knew that he could not silence them all before they reached the next plantation, and there were certainly other travelers on such a busy road at this time that could bear witness to his savage fury. He stood among the dead soldiers in silent disbelief. It had all happened so fast.

He had to clear his head for the coming challenge. It was no more than two hours hard ride to Baton Rouge, and the surviving troopers would certainly be hell bent on reaching the city as quickly as their mounts could take them. The furious Yankees would be back in force by midnight, looking for answers...and bent on revenge. Etenel Babako was in grave peril.

Chapter 20

Dumaine's Downfall

The wait would not be a long one; a full company of cavalry approached from the River Road, barely four hours from the time of the shootings and mayhem. The size of the column was an indication to Dumaine that this was to be a punitive expedition. He glared at them menacingly from his second floor balcony, then quickly changed his bullet ridden clothing and went downstairs to position himself on the front porch steps.

It was time for the curtain to rise on his grand performance, and he was well up to the challenge. Just as the lead riders reached the scene of the carnage, he rushed forward with a false limp, pointing a trembling finger in the direction of Algernon's assailants in the rear of the column.

"There they are....behind you, Colonel Harrington," he wailed with a quivering voice; "those are the men that murdered my overseer. Look at what they have done to him!" The colonel ordered a halt and dismounted, removing his gauntlets and placing his right hand over the flap of his sidearm in his holster as he strode forward with grim determination. Jack Harrington was a crusty old soldier, and not one to mince words.

"Murder, you say, my dear Mr. Dumaine. I have received quite a different story from my men. I will grant you the courtesy of an explanation before I arrest you and burn this plantation to the ground; now, out with it!"

185

"An..an explanation? Why, you can see plainly for yourself, colonel," Dumaine whined as he gestured pitifully at the bodies lying before them. "Those drunken soldiers invaded my property looking for a fight with imaginary Rebels; when they found none, my overseer ordered them off the grounds. They became belligerent, and it was then that they shot him in cold blood right where he lies now. See for yourself."

Dumaine noticed the hesitancy in the officer's face when he had mentioned the word "drunken" associated with the soldiers, so he continued along that path. "Were these men on orders from YOU to come here, Colonel Harrington? I cannot believe it to be so. You have been to my plantation before, both in an official and social capacity." He paused briefly for an assent, which the officer supplied with marked resignation.

"You know that I am loyal to the government of the United States in spite of my predicament here in a hostile country. I have taken the Oath, and yet this is how I am treated by the authorities sent here to protect me!"

The colonel was now the one on the defensive. Dumaine had planted the seeds of doubt, and they began to grow. "Of....of course I did not order them here," Harrington replied haltingly. His expression changed to one of embarrassment. "In truth, sir, the men were without any orders at all."

Dumaine feigned astonishment. "Do you mean that these soldiers abandoned their posts, then got liquored up, only to roam the countryside and wreak havoc on innocent citizenry?" He looked forlornly at Algernon. "Were there any other unfortunate incidents?"

"No, none at all!" the officer replied emphatically; "there were no other incidents. But according to my troopers, YOUR man opened fire without warning and killed two of them. Is that true?"

"Absolutely not, sir! My word of honor as a Christian gentleman! Come, come, Colonel; what one man would be foolish enough to take it upon himself to fire upon 12? My poor, loyal Algernon was defending me and my home, God bless his soul. These marauders were about to force their way into the mansion to search for supposedly hidden riches; when he denied them entry, they shot him down like a dog. Only great strength of will enabled him to return fire and kill those damned …foragers."

"They were going to ransack the house?" replied the colonel in a rising voice and widening eyes. "That IS news to me." He turned back towards the now sober accusers, who either looked away ashamedly, or stammered out weak, puppy like denials.

Harrington gave them a cold stare and returned to face Dumaine. "Sir," he said with a touch of embarrassment, "my men swear that you jumped from the upstairs balcony…like a wild animal onto trooper Whelan and broke his neck."

Dumaine paused for a moment of mock astonishment, and then laughed bitterly. "You must excuse my amusement under the circumstances, Colonel. The second floor balcony is nearly 20 feet away, not to mention 10 feet high. As you can plainly see, an old man stands before you. I will tell you what REALLY happened. In his drunken state, the soldier fell off his horse, landed hard on the ground at an odd angle, and…well, you can see the results for yourself."

Dumaine hunched over just a bit more to enhance his aged appearance. "I suppose that in their stupor, they also said they shot me." He stretched out his arms; "and yet, here I am, without a scratch on my body or a tear in my clothes, except for a glancing blow I took on my leg from a spooked horse during my head overseer's murder.

One of the original 12 troopers ran up to a corpse and stood pointing down at it. "Colonel, look here at Corporal Asprion's neck. That thing over there ripped him to pieces with his teeth! He ain't human, I tell ya."

"Colonel, if I may have a word with you privately, sir, that too can be readily explained," Dumaine said in a low voice as he took the now befuddled officer by the arm. The two men walked toward the front porch steps.

"It is painful for me to say this, colonel, but when the shooting started, the horses became understandably startled by the sudden burst of gunfire. In their drunkenness, the troopers could not properly control their mounts. The dead man in question bolted into the line of fire; subsequently, he was shot through the side of the neck by one of his own friends. Either they are hallucinating from strong Tennessee whiskey to come back to you with a story like that, or.....they are attempting to cover their own tracks."

Now Dumaine laid it on even thicker. "I believe that we have all suffered this day, Colonel. You cannot be held responsible for the actions of inebriated deserters, sir. No blame can be pointed in your direction. I am confident that as an officer and a gentleman you will see to the proper punishment for these men. I expect no less from a man of your integrity, sir, under the present circumstances"

Harrington stiffened up, wheeled around, and barked out orders with great annoyance. "Sergeant Kozlowski, place Rouse, Condon, and the others under arrest at once, then get a detail formed to remove these bodies. We are leaving immediately."

The Colonel turned back to Dumaine with a conciliatory tone. "Is there anything that I can possibly do for you here, sir? I can see to it that your man is given a proper burial wherever you desire."

"That is very gracious of you, colonel," Dumaine said dejectedly, "but I must attend to Algernon myself. He was a devoted, trusted employee, and a great friend; I will see that he is given a Christian burial here on the property that he tended and loved so well. It is the very least that I can do for him. He was a righteous, gentle, God fearing man. Now, if you would...please....leave me in peace. This has been a very distasteful experience."

"Your servant sir," Colonel Harrington replied as he saluted in appreciation for the plantation owner's great understanding and restraint. "This incident will not go unpunished, I can assure you."

Dumaine smiled approvingly as he watched the company ride off with the dead troopers tied and draped across the saddles of their horses. The ruse had worked to perfection; Etenel Babako was safe once more. He only wished that he could have killed a few more of those drunken blue bellies for depriving him of his head overseer.

While the immediate threat was gone, there was still much to do before daylight.

The first order of business was to choose a replacement for the faithful but flawed Algernon from among the remaining four overseers. They all feared him, so obedience would not be a stumbling block, and they treated the slaves shamelessly, something Dumaine expected from all the white men at Etenel Babako.

The individual needed to be one who could be trustworthy enough to manage the affairs of the plantation, and also safeguard Dumaine during those dangerous daylight hours when he was most vulnerable.

After considerable thought, Dumaine chose a young, lumbering giant of a man who simply went by the name of Guidry.

Although clearly not as bright as Algernon, he abused his position of power regularly, and thoroughly enjoyed inflicting pain, two fine traits for a head overseer. The fact that he was Cajun also appealed greatly to Dumaine. All that was needed was an introduction to the personal wants and needs of the master, a task that Dumaine would accomplish quite easily with his powers of persuasion.

Once the soldiers had left the vicinity, the remaining overseers emerged cautiously from the gray shadows and ventured out into the open. Dumaine wasted no time; it was then that the selection of Guidry was summarily announced. The dumbfounded hulk was instructed to continue operations for the coming day as scheduled, and then meet with Dumaine in the evening to discuss "other" issues.

Orders were also given to bury Algernon behind his former home and office. Several curious slaves were roused from their huts to perform the task of digging the grave; unlike most of their other labors, they performed this one with great, albeit concealed, pleasure.

There was no ceremony, no coffin, and no tears. With the night drawing to a close, Dumaine's time was also running out. He stayed momentarily to ensure that the proper location was selected, then left for the serenity of his bedroom before the burial took place. As he made his way to the main house he could not help but reveal his true inner thoughts.

"You were a fool, my impetuous Algernon; you truly could have cheated death. At the proper time, I would have rewarded you with eternal life. Now, you must meet your Maker with all the weight of your sins on your soul. I truly believe that the new accommodations HE has planned for you will not meet with your approval."

While the old night creature pondered over what might have been, the bloody, bullet ridden body of Algernon was wrapped in a filthy sheet and summarily dropped into the shallow grave. The ecstatic slaves quickly shoveled the dirt over their tormentor, then quietly danced and chanted with joy over the small earthen mound. There would be no headstone.

Dumaine returned wearily to the comfort of his rocker on the second floor balcony. He was intent on enjoying the last few hours before dawn in his favorite spot in the entire world. He sat gazing at the stars as the crickets chirped rhythmically in the orchards and bowling greens. The events of this night were indeed tumultuous, but he had weathered the storm in magnificent fashion, despite the crippling loss of Algernon. On the whole, he was quite pleased with himself and how things ended up.

The rest of the night passed much too quickly to suit Dumaine. Just when he was finally beginning to feel completely relaxed, the dawn began to make its presence known as it peeked out over the River Road. He was about to retire to the darkness of his shuttered bedroom when he heard the faint sounds of screams and shouts from behind the mansion. Soon the shouts grew louder; they were accompanied by the crackle of torches.

After a long minute, he looked down with disbelief at the sight of a large throng of screaming slaves below him and chanting the name of Joshua. With Algernon out of the way, the Negroes sensed that this was their moment to strike. They took full advantage of their strength in numbers; the terrified overseers were quickly overpowered and mercilessly butchered; then the bloody bodies were hoisted high in the air for Dumaine to witness. Other slaves carried axes and large, wooden crosses fashioned from garden hoes. The ends were sharpened to a fine point.

Their timing was superb. There were not even precious seconds for the old night creature to relocate to another safe haven. The hated dawn had arrived with all of its searing rays. Dumaine's existence had suddenly narrowed down to two possible choices. He could either flee to the momentary safety of his bedroom, where he would most certainly be staked and beheaded by the incensed darkies, or he could die gazing out over his beloved Etenel Babako.

Jacques Dumaine calmly chose to die with dignity. As he rocked slowly in his chair, the sun burned its way into his cold, dead flesh, setting his entire body on fire with a burst of red flame. The joyful slaves watching below gave thanks to the Lord for their deliverance.

Chapter 21

Victory and Retreat

On the very evening the drunken troopers began to hack their way along the main pathway within Etenel Babako, John Larson awoke in his warehouse hideaway on Railroad Street to the overpowering stench of rotting meat. He began to gag, but was sure to cover his mouth in an effort to avoid revealing his exact location. The smell meant only one thing; Freemasons had discovered his presence and were searching for him nearby.

He inched the black tarp that covered him slowly downward until his eyes were free to observe his immediate surroundings. There seemed to be neither sound nor movement in the large stall he had chosen for his day's rest; that at least gave him some initial relief. Rising to his feet, he made a run for the building entrance's sliding double doors, but as John reached the center of the warehouse, he was brought to his knees by clumps of garlic thrown from all directions.

"THAT WILL BE FAR ENOUGH, FILTH," a hate filled voice boomed piously. "This is the END of your miserable existence!" John whirled around to see that seven soldiers had him surrounded; they were moving slowly forward in an ever shrinking circle.

"Of course," John whispered with disgust. "Seven of them...the magical number of the Freemasons. They are so predictable with their mumbo jumbo." All were officers, five Union and two Confederate. It was as Dumaine had prophesized; the race of men did not care whose side he took; their only concern was his extinction from this earth.

"Do not think that you can fly from this trap, filth," one Federal spoke ominously. "The flat roof of this warehouse has afforded us the opportunity of placing garlic where it is needed most. There will be no escape from the air to foil our mission."

"I too have a mission," John replied to him in an almost pleading tone. "I have come to aid YOUR CAUSE. Already I have damaged the Rebel army, and I can do more, much more. Once we have secured a victory here, I can go on to Richmond and dispatch Jefferson Davis, his cabinet, whomever I please. All I ask for is the opportunity to continue my work until the war is won and the Union is preserved; then I will be on my way."

"No," the Yankee officer replied as he shook his head evenly back and forth. "If we are to win this war, it will be the result of God's will; only then shall the ground become blessed by the sacred blood of our honored dead. Your interference has here has fouled their sacrifice. There is no place in the world for such a loathsome creature as you. HERE you will die." The grim faced men inched closer.

"How did you learn of my presence?" John asked incredulously.

"One of the Rebel generals you attacked was a Freemason; he was wounded and taken to my field hospital, where I noticed the bite marks on his neck while I tended to him before his death. It was then that we knew that there was a VAMPIRE among us."

One of the Confederate officers, whom John assumed was a prisoner, chimed in. "I had an inkling before that. Three of my men were found dead under suspicious circumstances a few days ago just west of Gettysburg; one picket had his neck snapped, while two of General Hill's headquarter sentries had their skulls crushed and then their bodies hidden."

The Rebel waited for some sign of acknowledgement from John, but he was not given that satisfaction; he went on. "Guards are surprised and killed in any number of ways, but this was too far out of the ordinary. No one else in camp was harmed, and nothing was stolen or destroyed."

John pictured the listless General Hill sprawled on the bed in his room of the hotel. There was no mention of him, or the other four gray clad officers he had chosen for special attention. That was good news.

The seven men held the weapons that threatened their adversary's survival—crosses, stakes, axes, garlic, and bottles with what John presumed to be water that had been blessed. One man's uniform was black in color. That could only mean he was a clergyman. They had come well prepared, these Freemasons, and they seemed determined to make good use of the arsenal at their disposal.

No, there would be no reasoning with these mortals. The Rebel concluded: "You are an abomination to the Supreme Being; it is our solemn duty to destroy you. We are ALL foresworn to this one purpose. The war cannot change that."

John knew at that moment all discussion was at an end. He sprang at his tormentor with a speed that took everyone by surprise. The Rebel raised an axe in a futile effort to swipe off John's head, but it was too late. In an instant, the man's throat had been ripped open; he fell backwards onto the ground and flailed about, chortling up blood and gasping for whatever last breaths he could muster.

John then felt a searing pain on his face and neck, while his cold flesh sizzled with an unbearable heat. The clergyman had thrown holy water on him in an attempt to stave off the attack. It was the last thing he would do. John grabbed him in a bear hug and bit deeply into his the side of his neck, sucking with a force so powerful that the officer seemed to shrivel into a mocking shell. Having no desire to make the shaman a fellow creature, John stopped his feed and shoved his hand through the man's stomach, ripping out whatever internal organs he could find. There was not even time enough for a scream.

A third man lunged from behind, drove a stake into John's back near the left shoulder blade and straight through to the other side. But his thrust missed the heart by a mere half an inch; John staggered for a moment, and then spun around to confront his impaler. The remaining Confederate rushed from the side and placed a silver crucifix along the wounded night creature's head, which brought a howl of agony.

John grabbed him by his uniform shirt and flung him head over heels into a nearby retaining wall, initiating a dull smacking sound as the body dropped to the floor in a lifeless heap of twisted arms and legs. That left four Freemasons, who despite the proper weaponry at their disposal, were now wavering and overcome with fear.

John could smell that fear as it intermingled with their garlic. He grasped the point of the stake sticking out the front of his chest and pulled it through until it was free of his body. He threw it to the floor with a vengeance, and then reached up to rub the hole that had come ever so close to his heart. There was no blood, and the pain would linger for only a short time. The drained Freemason cleric had provided John with the strength to heal quickly. He faced the last attackers with a look of sadness and resignation on his face.

"This did not have to happen. I told you....I am here to support your cause. These deaths are on you and your secret brethren everywhere. I will spare your life. Go, tell them to leave me in peace until this war is won, then I will be gone from your midst... tell them."

The soldiers backed away until they reached the front of the warehouse. When they felt that they were at a safe distance, the four turned and sprinted for their mounts. As they sped off into the distance, one of them stopped, wheeled his horse about, and let out a final warning. "It is not over. We will find you and send you to the depths of hell; I SWEAR IT!"

John lowered his head and hunched over in dismay. He muttered sadly to himself: "Dumaine, Dumaine, how right you were. Why must they hate us so?" He walked slowly out of the warehouse, fully expecting to hear the sounds of another great battle winding down. He was surprised to hear nothing of the sort. In fact, the night was devoid of any noises military in nature; rather, the rhythmic patter of a pelting rain emanated from the countryside.

Just what was going on between the two opposing armies? Situated in and around Gettysburg were well over 165,000 soldiers. Could it be that there had been no resumption of hostilities for an entire day? Something was just not right, and John was determined to find out the cause of this surreal outbreak of peace. Perhaps cooler heads had finally prevailed, and the respective governments had called for a cease fire. John hoped that was the case, but ultimately, his knowledge of human nature quickly snapped him out of that dream.

The night before he had scouted the lines of the Army of Northern Virginia; tonight, when total darkness had settled in, he would do the same for his Army of the Potomac. While he waited patiently on the floor of the warehouse beside the dead soldiers, John inexplicably could not prevent his mind from returning to thoughts of Dumaine and his beautiful plantation.

He sorely missed his mentor and the safe surroundings of Etenel Babako; he suddenly had a strange, frightening sensation that something was very wrong back in Louisiana, but there was nothing that he could do about it now. Algernon and Dumaine would have to handle whatever situation was causing his anxiety. John wished that he could be back there to help them, but he was on a more important mission. The survival of his country meant more to him than the continued existence of his kind.

He took to the skies around 10PM and traveled to Little Round Top, the shank end of the inverted fish hook line that the Federals had made several days ago. Union soldiers were there all right, but in greater numbers than before. Working his way north, blue troops were still firmly dug in along Cemetery Ridge, Cemetery Hill, and Culp's Hill as well.

It seemed as though the Federal commander had done nothing but fortify, content to wait for another strike from the Confederates. However, strictly from a numbers and morale standpoint, another attack certainly would not be reasonable, even for the audacious Lee. His army had been badly mauled on that Emmitsburg Road killing field. It did not appear, at least from John's observations while in their camp, that the Rebels could have any powerful offensive capability remaining.

Ironically, attempting to gather pertinent information could prove more difficult to obtain behind the Union lines for John. As a ragtag Rebel, he blended in perfectly with their troops; as a Yankees, it would be a different story. Everyone but the teamsters seemed clad in a blue uniform. While he thought about milling behind the lines as a wagon driver, there would be only so many places he could linger without attracting undue attention, and he needed to be even more careful now that his presence was known to both sides.

John decided to light down at one of the many field hospitals that dotted the countryside along the Federal entrenchments. He followed the Tanneytown Road north up to Evergreen Cemetery; just to the west were the Trostle Farm and the nearby VI Corps Hospital. Unfortunately, the situation of the wounded there was not much different than the butcher shop that he had encountered behind the enemy's lines.

It was a ghastly reprise. There were the mounds of amputated limbs fresh from the surgeons' bloody saws, and scores of moaning men lay on the ground devoid of any forms of cover. Wafting above it all was the unmistakable, lingering smell of pus and decay, while the occasional death rattle signaled a further thinning of the ranks.

John squatted down beside a makeshift tent and listened in on the sporadic banter and conversations of the wounded. He crossed his arms and lowered his chin to his breast while pulling his hat down to his nose in an effort to feign sleep.

"I was with General Gibbon on Cemetery Ridge when the Rebs attacked in force on the 3rd," one private said to another as he delicately patted the stump that was his left leg. "I was scared, mighty scared; but by God, it was such a beautiful sight to behold." He paused for a moment in reflection.

"Those Johnnies started marching through the open field like it was some dad blasted Sunday dress parade. Even when our artillery opened up and cut down hundreds of em' in the ranks, they stayed in marching formation and dressed their lines like it was a summer breeze a blowin'. An' some of their officers had the sand to advance on horseback!! Talk about pretty targets to choose from…got to tip my hat to all those brave boys."

"I was with General McIntosh's Brigade on the Hanover Road," the other soldier replied wearily. "Jus' like we thought, the Reb cavalry was tryin' to turn our flank and attack us from the rear. We charged each other over and over again; seemed like a hundred times to me. There was a lot of yellin' an' shootin' an' slashin' away, but they finally gave up and headed back toward the ridge."

He waved his right wrist, which was minus its hand. "That's how I lost this. I was squarin' off with this Reb officer, see, an' he slices my hand off with his saber as easy as you please, jus' before I can take a bead on him with my pistol."

He sighed and continued on. "He let me go, though; coulda killed me if he was so inclined, but I was a screamin' an a bleedin' like a stuck pig. Guess he plumb felt sorry for me. I woulda liked to thank him for that, lettin' me live, that is. Hope he made it back to his lines all right… know what I mean?"

"Yup," his companion said wistfully as he closed his eyes briefly. "That I do."

John began a criss-cross about the hospital grounds as much as he dared, but he could not gather much current battlefield information, except to find out that the Army of the Potomac was being led by Major General George Meade, a native Pennsylvanian, and another of the many West Point graduates serving on both sides in the war.

"Meade," John remarked to himself. "I guess everyone had seen enough of General Hooker after Chancellorsville. Only the devil would know where they find these incompetent fools. Perhaps this Meade fellow will provide the necessary leadership and vision necessary for complete victory."

The evening was passing by quickly with little to show for it, save for a slackening off of the rain; John felt it was time to move on. Stretching up and walking into a small stand of oaks, he took flight and went due east, passed the Taneytown Road, Cemetery Hill, the Baltimore Pike, and finally, Culp's Hill. At the southeast side of the hill was the Spangler Farm, near Rock Creek. This was the site of the XI Corps Hospital.

John had learned something else this night; neither the Union nor Confederate army medical staffs were prepared to deal with the number of casualties on such a monstrous scale. The wounded seemed to be almost an afterthought, like unwanted leaves scattered about the landscape. There were not enough surgical doctors, orderlies, nurses, stretcher bearers, ambulances, bandages, chloroform; the list was truly endless, and many a good man from the North and South would die unnecessarily because of it.

John picked up a small crate of weevil filled hardtack and began a slow walk around the campfires. This would be as good a cover as any, delivering much needed food. He stopped behind a tent and proceeded to sort through the crate; two junior officers sat on camp stools on the other side and were engaged in conversation. Perhaps this would be a good spot to pick up some news. He listened in attentively.

"The Old Snapping Turtle's done a fine job for us thus far. I wouldn't have believed it after the first day, but our boys held. I half hoped that they would have come at us one more time."

"Yes," replied the other officer, "I think Lee expected Meade and the rest of us to break and run again. Funny, now they're the ones running, maybe all the way back to Virginia."

"What do you mean?"

"Our cavalry reported that a long line of wagons and ambulances were headed west over the Chambersburg Pike through Fairfield Gap, probably filled with what's left of their supplies and wounded. The rest of the Reb army is trekking through Monterey Pass; pretty slow going with all this mud and rain."

"That's a good sign. What about their prisoners? They bagged a lot of us in the retreat through the town."

"I heard some Reb officer came over with a flag of truce yesterday to try and parlay an exchange, but Meade told him no. Can you believe it?"

"The general's a crafty old soldier. He knows it'll be harder on the Rebs in their retreat if they have to keep a guard on a heap of prisoners; might even slow them down enough for us to catch up."

"That's not happening."

"And why not? We've got them on the run; now's the time to chop them up, while they're strung out in long columns."

"Our boys have taken a good beating too the past three days. Meade thinks it's best to get our strength back before we head out after them. Supplies are on the way; plus...you never know what General Lee's got up his sleeve. Maybe he WANTS us to follow them. Maybe he's set a trap for us. The REBS are the ones that have abandoned the field this time. This victory belongs to the Army of the Potomac. No need to give some of it back."

"Seems a damn shame to let them sneak off for home, though, just so they can refit and hit us again some other time. I'm no general, and probably never will be, but it's my opinion that if we can whip the Army of Northern Virginia once and for all, then the Confederacy's done for, too."

"You're right; you'll never be a general. Let's get something to eat. I haven't had a bite since breakfast."

John took the cue and walked up to the officers with the crate of his weevil infested hard tack and offered them some. They peeked down hopefully inside the crate, then one of the officers sighed deeply.

"Why is it that we can never get a meal that stays still?"

Bugs notwithstanding, they sorted through and picked out the biscuits they wanted, thanked John for the bountiful repast, and walked off in a final exchange.

"Don't worry; we'll follow standard military procedure--brew some coffee and throw in the hardtack. The weevils'll swim to the top, and then we can scoop em' out and eat the biscuits without those pesky little critters inside."

"Good plan of action; a textbook response. You know something... I was dead wrong. You WILL be a general someday."

John had struck a gold mine of information. He now knew that Lee was in nearly full retreat mode. He continued walking, thinking of the previous conversation, and stopping to hand out hard tack. What ABOUT attacking the Confederates now, when they were most vulnerable? It seemed a capital idea. Despite their bravery, they were still the enemy; they HAD to be annihilated to restore the United States.

Just then, John came upon two battered troopers propped up against a fallen log. They were gently tending to each other's wounds.

One was a Union soldier, with a bloody bandage over his head; he had been hit by shrapnel. The other was a Confederate, with his right arm in a muddy, makeshift sling, courtesy of a mini ball. The bullet had gone clean through the fleshy part of his arm and missed the bone. He considered himself extremely lucky.

"Well, Johnny, you gotta admit, we took it to you this time."

The Rebel shook his head in agreement. "Lordy, you surely did."

"It was like Fredericksburg all over again, only....in reverse this time."

"Yur right about that. I was behind the stone wall at Marye's Heights that cold December day. Never thought it would happen to us. Seemed like murder to me at the time. Still does, I reckon." There was a long pause.

"You need anything, Johnny?"

"My arm's a throbbin'."

"I'll move things around for you. Sing out when it's ok." The Union man adjusted the sling, and his companion nodded his head when all was well again. "There you go, friend."

"Thanks, Yank. Sure wish I'd a met you afore this damned war started. Seems a shame, us killin' each other an all."

"That it do, Reb. That it do.....Hell, let's try to get some sleep. Looks like the sun may be up in a bit."

John watched the interaction of the two men with total fascination. For them, any just causes for this war now seemed so wrong, but like the millions of soldiers involved in it, they knew that they was duty bound to play out their little part, come what may. It was as if they were all being manipulated by some greater power like so many string puppets bobbing up and down into a mixture of blood and tears.

He left the case of hard tack with a grateful nurse, and after reaching the woods, he took to the skies, making his way onto the flat roof of the spacious, red brick gatehouse of the Evergreen Cemetery situated just off the Baltimore Pike. Union artillery batteries were positioned in front and on both sides. Amazingly enough, the grand structure had escaped relatively unscathed, in spite of the fact that it was one of the most enticing targets on the entire battlefield.

John looked anxiously to the west; the tattered Confederates WERE in full retreat and headed for the welcomed safety of Virginia! The immediate threat was over; enemy forces had been repulsed from the soil of Pennsylvania by the resurgent Army of the Potomac, and the frightened citizenry and politicians in Washington could breathe a sigh of relief.

The night creature turned Union avenger stood defiantly on the top edge on the gatehouse roof, debating whether or not to trail in the wake of the battered Rebels and hack away at the weakened, bleeding army. It would be a simple task, but he had a strong feeling that he would not be alone. The disguised specter of Death would be dutifully moving among the scream-filled ambulance wagons to collect his due, while the relentless Vampire Council would be nipping at his heels with a vengeance.

It was then that John cast a quick glance over his shoulder to the east. Any final decision would have to wait until the following evening. There was a small break in the clouds, and the sun was slowly beginning to rise; but for this one day at least, there would be a blue dawn over Gettysburg.

Epilogue

Pertinent historical information pursuant to the Confederate generals "disabled" in this story:

Lieutenant General Ambrose Powell Hill was the Commanding Officer, 3rd Corps, Confederate Army of Northern Virginia. It has been written that he was greatly debilitated by what has tactfully been characterized as a "chronic illness" during the time of the battle of Gettysburg. He headquartered at the Cashtown Hotel, which still stands today as a bed and breakfast. It is purported to be haunted.

Later investigations have revealed that he suffered from gonorrhea, courtesy of a pre-war trip to New York City; (what a surprise). This was a malady that more often than not resulted in slow death due to the inadequate state of 19th century medicine. A sudden, temporary blood loss might also have incapacitated him. Whatever the real reason for his weakened condition, one of the Rebel army's three veteran corps commanders was physically and mentally unfit for duty, a situation that certainly would have hampered Lee's offensive initiatives while in enemy territory.

Little Powell, as Hill was also called, was known to wear a red calico shirt just prior to engagements with the enemy to show disdain for his own safety. It would become known as his "battle shirt." The general's health continued its steady decline after the battle of Gettysburg, and he was often unable to adequately fulfill his duties as a corps commander. He was shot and killed during the siege of Petersburg in April of 1865, one week before Lee formally surrendered the Army of Northern Virginia.

Lieutenant General Richard Ewell was the Commanding Officer, 2nd Corps, Confederate Army of Northern Virginia. He lost his left leg during The Battle of Second Manassas, and then returned to duty, eventually replacing the late Stonewall Jackson just about the time of the Gettysburg campaign.

The profoundly profane Ewell had been the pious Jackson's most reliable subordinate; thus they were truly an odd couple. He learned valuable first hand lessons from "Old Jack" on the art of striking an opponent off guard, and following up an enemy's rout with vigorous pursuit.

In spite of this previous training, Ewell exhibited an uncharacteristic bout of indecisiveness during the battle; perhaps this was due in part to his outhouse encounter while encamped at Heidlersburg. His critical decision not to attack the desperate, regrouping Federals on Cemetery Hill in the late afternoon of July 1st brought howls of protest from a number of his fellow officers.

Ewell's hesitancy and inability to comprehend the importance of the situation is looked upon by some historians as one of the key turning points in the battle. His health slowly declined to the point where he was relieved of his duties in the Army of Northern Virginia and reassigned to the Department of Richmond two years later. He survived the war and died of pneumonia in 1872.

Brigadier General Lewis Armistead of Pickett's Division, 1st Corps, Army of Northern Virginia is best known for his valiant efforts in the famous, or infamous, Pickett's  Charge on Day #3. He heroically lead a group of about 200 Virginians through center of the Federal line on Cemetery Ridge at what is now called the "angle" despite a total absence of follow up support. He was shot in the right arm and left knee as the Rebel breach was quickly sealed by Union reinforcements.

While lying disabled on the ground, Armistead cried out that he was the "son of a widow," a cryptic phrase signifying to anyone within earshot that he was a Freemason. His message was overheard, and he was tended to by fellow Mason Captain Henry Bingham of the Union's Second Corps.

Despite the fact that neither of his wounds was life threatening, he inexplicably died of exhaustion two days later at the 11th Corps field hospital on the George Spangler farm. Perhaps the additional blood siphoned the night before the charge made a bad situation worse? The general was affectionately called "Lo" by his close friends. He was a member of Alexandria-Washington Masonic Lodge #22.

Lieutenant General James Longstreet was the Commanding Officer, 1st Corps, Confederate Army of Northern Virginia. A large, well built man who looked the part of a soldier, Longstreet was also Robert E.

Lee's most trusted military advisor in the field, so much so that Lee affectionately referred to him as "My Old War Horse." However, during the battle of Gettysburg, the two men clashed repeatedly over strategy and tactics, particularly Lee's decision to launch Pickett's Charge on Day #3.

It has been suggested by his lethargic actions on July 3rd that Longstreet either would not, or could not, give a wholehearted effort to the grand charge. It was his overriding belief that the Army of Northern Virginia should have followed the tactical defensive while in Pennsylvania, and it was his professional opinion that the attack on the third day would fail.

Longstreet was incessantly gored in print after the war by Confederate officers who blamed him directly for the defeat at Gettysburg. He gained the ultimate revenge by outliving nearly all of them, and he died in 1904 at the age of 82. To this day, many Lee apologists continue to claim that it was Longstreet's pouting and subsequent sluggishness that was the real reason for the disjointed failure of the massive thrust directed at the center of the Union line on Cemetery Ridge; but what if his strength had been sapped the night before?

Robert E. Lee was the Commanding General, Confederate Army of Northern Virginia. He is often referred to as the "Marble Man" as a result of his impeccable comportment, impressive victories, and the

unprecedented feat of being the only cadet in the glorious history of West Point to graduate without a single demerit.

The battle of Gettysburg, however, has been labeled as Lee's worst effort of the entire Civil War. His decisions and reactions to events over the course of battle, particularly on Day #3, suggest that he may have been physically and or mentally exhausted. It has come to light that Lee suffered from a serious heart ailment, with signs pointing towards angina pectoris, a coronary artery disease. This may have been the root cause of his missteps, perhaps with a bit of latent instruction to his subconscious?

Chest pains that he experienced at Fredericksburg six months earlier may very well have been a mild heart attack from which he never fully recovered. Lee would eventually die of heart failure in 1870 at age 63 while president of Washington College in Lexington, Virginia. Upon his death, the school was renamed Washington and Lee University.

Author's Notes

The Freemasons are members of an ancient, secret society that espouse brotherhood, mutual assistance, the pursuit of knowledge, and a belief in a Supreme Being. The order continues practicing good public works to this very day, although the actual meaning of many of the society's rituals has been lost to time. The Freemasons emphasis on secrecy has spawned a variety of conspiracy theories relative to their real intentions.

The most prevalent theory, passionately espoused by the usual suspect left wing hysterics, is that the Freemasons are bound and determined to rule the world via their vast unseen political and economic clout. Homer Simpson also claimed that the Masons successfully blocked the United States from adopting the metric system.

One of the most familiar symbols of Freemasonry is an intersecting square and compass, found alternately with and without a large letter "G" in the center, which some say stands for God. The never ending battle with vampires as depicted in this book is fictional. Close to 18,000 Freemasons from the North and South fought in the battle of Gettysburg; of that number, 5,600 of them were either killed, wounded, or listed as missing in action.

Djadadjii was the name given to the olden days vampire hunters of Bulgaria. According to legend, these men would lure a vampire from its lair with some blood placed inside a glass bottle. Once out in the open, the creature was subsequently shape shifted and forced into the bottle by the djadadjii with the aid of religious icons. The bottle was then quickly corked shut and thrown into a bonfire. The night creatures' special "Council" was a spin off based upon these hunters. Please feel free to stumble like a drunken sailor on shore leave over the phonetic pronunciation of djadadjii all you like. I believe that only Eastern Europeans can say the word properly.

Limitations often hampered the impressive array of supernatural powers possessed by vampires. One of the least known restrictions was their annoying inability (at least from the vampires point of view), to cross the threshold of a house without a verbal invitation from someone inside. Of course, if said permission could be obtained through trickery, as it often was, then everyone in the home was fair game, in the most literal sense

Brigadier General Alexander Schimmelfennig was the Commanding Officer of the 1st Brigade, 3rd Division, 11th Corps, Union Army of the Potomac. This undistinguished general became cut off during the retreat through Gettysburg during Day #1 of the battle. He successfully, or shamelessly, hid amongst the Confederates for three days in the combination woodshed/

pigsty behind the home of Henry and Catherine Garlach while Federal forces made their impressive defensive stand.

Mrs. Garlach personally provided the general with food and kept his hiding place a secret. Unfortunately (for the Union), he was never killed or captured, and Schimmelfennig returned to duty after Confederates forces withdrew from the town. He survived the war with an uninspiring service record, but died in the fall of 1865 from tuberculosis.

Horatio S. Howell was the chaplain of the 90th Pennsylvania Infantry Regiment. He was shot and killed July 1st on the outside top step of Gettysburg's Christ Lutheran Church when he refused to surrender his sword to a Confederate soldier passing by the makeshift hospital inside the church during the midst of the Union retreat through the town. The church still stands, sans blood, complete with a bronze plaque on its front steps honoring the sacrifice of Chaplain Howell.

Major General George Pickett was the Division Commander of the 1st Corps, Confederate Army of Northern Virginia. Arguably a bit of a dandy, he was usually well dressed, and often scented his curled hair with perfume. At the time of the battle of Gettysburg, he was smitten by the charms of one Sallie Corbell, a young, Southern belle whom he eventually married several months after the battle.

Although he was a brave soldier, he was a less than stellar general. He is chiefly remembered to history as a result of "Picket's Charge," the ill-fated movement of July 3rd that directed 12,500 of his men towards the center of the Union line on Cemetery Ridge; only half of the Confederates would return unscathed to the safety of Seminary

Ridge.

He never forgave Lee for issuing the order that destroyed his division, and the two men endured a strained relationship after the war. Pickett died in 1875, whereupon his faithful widow Sallie took up the gauntlet and penned some very flattering books about her late husband; unfortunately, much of what she has written can now kindly be categorized as unreliable public relations spin. He too was, yes, you guessed it, a Freemason, and member of Dove's Lodge #51 in Richmond.

Mary Virginia "Ginny" Wade, John's brief unrequited love interest, has the dubious honor of being the only civilian to be killed during the battle of Gettysburg. The 20 year old woman was shot in the back by a Confederate sharpshooter early on July 3rd while she was making bread for Union soldiers in the kitchen of her sister's home on Baltimore Street. Her lifeless body was brought temporarily to the basement; that area of the house is now said to be haunted. The home has since been refurbished and is a popular though tacky tourist attraction.

There has been some speculation that she was engaged to another

Gettysburg resident, Corporal Johnston "Jack" Skelly, Jr. of the 87th Pennsylvania Volunteer Infantry, who died soon after Ginny from wounds received during the battle of Winchester. The two are buried near one another in Gettysburg's Evergreen Cemetery.

As a result of a typographical error from a period newspaper story recording her death, she has gone down in history as "Jennie" Wade.

Mary Thompson lived in a small, two-story stone house on the Chambersburg Pike during the summer of 1863. Known around Gettysburg as the "Widow" Thompson, this feisty Unionist was in her late 60's when she had the dubious distinction of having her dwelling utilized as a field headquarters during the battle by

none other than Robert E. Lee himself. While only temporary, she was decidedly unhappy with those domestic arrangements. The episode with General Lee depicted in the story is fictional. Subsequent questions posed to Mary by curious visitors after the battle as to whether she actually cooked any meals for the general were usually met with icy denials. (Thank you to General Lee's Headquarters Museum, Gettysburg, PA for the picture of Mary Thompson.)

Marie Laveau, the undisputed queen of voodoo, but also a devout Catholic, was a free woman of mixed color, and the most feared, revered, and recognized voodooienne of 19th Century New Orleans. It was said that she could help or hurt anyone she desired with her odd blending of secretive West African and Roman Catholic religious rituals.

Despite her powers, she died quietly in the Crescent City in 1881 at the age of 87; visitors still frequent her grave in St Louis Cemetery #1 near the French Quarter and leave her offerings such as flowers and food in return for the granting of their fondest wishes. Hey, it may not help, but it can't hurt. The New Orleans "Coffee House" briefly mentioned in the story still stands today as The Old Absinthe House, a very popular watering hole for both locals and tourists alike.

The Agricultural College of Pennsylvania was the precursor to present day Penn State University, although its original name was Farmers High School of Pennsylvania. The "Old Main" was the principal structure at the college grounds, and it still remains a fixture at the University. Dr. Evan Pugh was an agricultural chemist who became its first President.

The Harriet Beecher Stowe novel recollected briefly by John was Uncle Tom's Cabin, or Life Among the Lowly, as it was also called. An anti-slavery story published in 1852, it introduced hundreds of thousands of Americans to the evils associated with the South's "peculiar institution," and the book fanned the flames of sectional discord well into the 1860's. Abolitionists also made good use of it to foster their cause.

Robert Rhett was a famous "fire brand" aristocrat from South Carolina. A United States Congressman and Senator prior to the outbreak of the war, Rhett's secessionist/extremist political views continued to shine on in the national spotlight mainly via his articles and stories in The Charleston Mercury, an influential 1860's Southern paper that was highly regarded for its war news and political editorials.

The **Oath of Allegiance** was a wartime loyalty pledge to the United States; it was taken by those citizens in Federal occupied Southern states who professed to remain faithful to the Union. The oath allowed plantation owners to keep their slaves, and ensured that their crops and homes would be neither destroyed nor confiscated. This was a pretty good deal, so people lied of course.

Henry Harrison was a purported pre-war actor turned Confederate spy in the employment of Lieutenant General James Longstreet. It was his startling information in late June of 1863 pursuant to the Army of the Potomac's movement north that made Lee concentrate his previously scattered forces. His contributions finally received widespread notoriety in the film "Gettysburg."

The **River Road** is the name of a 70 odd mile stretch of Greek Revival, French Creole, Italianesque, and French Colonial plantation homes that stood proudly on either side of the Mississippi River in southeast Louisiana, between Baton Rouge and New Orleans during the 19th century. Many of them were subsequently lost to the ravages of time. Fortunately, the breathtaking homes mentioned in the story by the character of Lucinda were saved and restored.

They are now popular tourist attractions, and examples of an opulent lifestyle that is reminiscent of Tara in "Gone with the Wind." Conversely, Evergreen Plantation in Wallace, Louisiana is unique in that it still retains rows of wooden slave shacks on site; a striking reminder of the oft used phrase all that glitters is not gold.

Lincoln's "sneaking disguised" into Washington, mentioned briefly by the pompous Dixie riverboat businessman, was a reference to the President's inglorious and secret arrival to the capital in February of 1861 for his upcoming inauguration. Death threats had forced him to abandon hopes for a triumphant journey from Springfield. Instead, Alan Pinkerton, who was to later form the now famous Pinkerton Detective Agency, convinced Lincoln to arrive unannounced and without fanfare.

Lincoln's night train pulled into the capital in the early morning hours, and he was taken swiftly to Willard's Hotel with only his friend Ward Hill Lamon and Pinkerton in tow. When word of this got out, the future President was excoriated in the press, particularly in the South, where he was caricatured as wearing a shawl and a cap pulled down low as a disguise.

Gettysburg was founded by the Scottish-Irish Gettys family in the late 1780's. Located about 40 miles south and west of Harrisburg, the state capital, Gettysburg was a thriving community with a population of 2,400 in July of 1863, courtesy of the 10 roads that led into it from all directions. Despite the fact that 165,000 soldiers fought long and hard in and around the town for three days, Gettysburg itself sustained only minor damage from shot and shell, with just one civilian fatality, the aforementioned Jenny Wade.

However, the town was overwhelmed with casualties from both sides; public buildings, churches, and private homes were used as temporary hospitals to aid the wounded during and after the battle, while on a more pragmatic note, thousands of dead men and horses required burial as quickly as possible. Land was purchased shortly thereafter to establish a National Cemetery for interment of the soldiers, and on November 19, 1863, President Lincoln gave what is now known as his famous "Gettysburg Address."

The **Evergreen Cemetery Gatehouse**, grand entrance to Gettysburg's "other" cemetery, was a silent witness to the battle of Gettysburg. Despite being a delicious target for Confederate artillerists,

the sturdy brick building, which also doubled as the caretaker's house, would emerge largely unscathed from the three day ordeal of shot and shell.

It has proudly withstood the ravages of time, and is maintained through the Evergreen Cemetery Association's Capital Improvement Fund. (Contributions are tax deductible; call: 717 334 4121).

The REAL John Larson is the flesh and blood Deputy Commissioner for The City of White Plains, NY, Department of Parking; he is also a good friend. Despite not knowing how he would be portrayed, he foolishly gave his blessing for the use of his name, and thus became the model for the main character in this book. Thanks John.

General Order Number One:
To Any Civil War Enthusiasts Who Might Read This Book

Blue Dawn Over Gettysburg is meant as a fang in cheek variation on what serious scholars have preached pursuant to the clash that was arguably the most important of all Civil War battles. I have made an honest effort to stick to the actual timeline, events, and characters as they have been popularly portrayed before inserting my own peculiar twists. However, if I have stumbled historically somewhere along the way, please don't break out the double canister. Some Civil War buffs can be way too serious.

Credit for pictures: Thank you to General Lee's Headquarters Museum, Gettysburg, PA for the picture of Mary Thompson. All additional pictures included in the Epilogue and Authors Notes are in the public domain, and many can be found through the Library of Congress.

Reference Sources

The American Civil War – 365 Days, by Margaret E. Wagner. (2006)

The Battle of Gettysburg, by Harry Pfanz, Scott Hartwig, and George Skoch, (1994)

Chronicles of the Civil War, by David Phillips and John C. Wideman, (1999)

The Civil War, by Geoffrey Ward, Rick Burns, and Ken Burns, (1990)

Days of Uncertainty and Dread, by Gerald Bennett, (1997)

Delta Sugar, by John Rehder, (1999)

The Divided Union, by Peter Batty and Peter Parish, (1987)

The Encyclopedia of the American Civil War, edited by David and Jen Heidler, (2000)

Freemasons—Inside the World's Oldest Secret Society, by Paul Jeffers, (2005)

Gangrene and Glory, by Frank R. Freemon, (2001)

Gettysburg, the Confederate High Tide, by Champ Clark, (1985)

The Gettysburg Campaign, a Study in Command, by Edwin Coddington, (1968)

Louisiana Plantation Homes, the Grace and Grandeur, by Joe Arrigo and Dick Dietrich, (1991)

Louisiana Real and Rustic, by Emeril Lagasse and Marcelle Bienvenue, (1996)

The Majesty of the River Road, by Paul Malone and Lee Malone, (2001)

Railroads of the Nineteenth Century, edited by Robert Frey, (1988)

Secret Lives of the Civil War, by Cormac O'Brien, (2007)

The Story of Lee's Headquarters, by Timothy H. Smith, (1995)

A Vast Sea of Misery, by Gregory Coco, (1988)

The Vampire Book—Encyclopedia of the Undead, by Gordon Melton, (1999)

Witness to Gettysburg, by Richard Wheeler, (1987)

ISBN 142516748-9

9 781425 167486